America Street A Multicultural Anthology...

AMERICA STREET

OTHER PERSEA ANTHOLOGIES

GOING WHERE I'M COMING FROM: MEMOIRS OF AMERICAN YOUTH
Edited by Anne Mazer

WORKING DAYS: SHORT STORIES ABOUT TEENAGERS AT WORK
Edited by Anne Mazer

A WALK IN MY WORLD: INTERNATIONAL SHORT STORIES ABOUT YOUTH
Edited by Anne Mazer

FIRST SIGHTINGS: CONTEMPORARY STORIES OF AMERICAN YOUTH
Edited by John Loughery

INTO THE WIDENING WORLD: INTERNATIONAL COMING-OF-AGE STORIES
Edited by John Loughery

STARTING WITH "I": PERSONAL ESSAYS BY TEENAGERS
by Youth Communication
Edited by Andrea Estepa and Philip Kay

THE HEART KNOWS SOMETHING DIFFERENT:
TEENAGE VOICES FROM THE FOSTER CARE SYSTEM
by Youth Communication
Edited by Al Desetta

SHOW ME A HERO: GREAT CONTEMPORARY STORIES ABOUT SPORTS
Edited by Jeanne Schinto

VIRTUALLY NOW: STORIES OF SCIENCE, TECHNOLOGY, AND THE FUTURE
Edited by Jeanne Schinto

AMERICA STREET

A MULTICULTURAL ANTHOLOGY OF STORIES

Edited by Anne Mazer

A Karen and Michael Braziller Book
PERSEA BOOKS / NEW YORK

Many people gave me invaluable assistance in compiling *America Street*. Robert Kane of the New York City School Volunteer Program, Inc. told us there was a need for this book. Karen Braziller, the editorial director of Persea Books, worked closely with me throughout the project. Thanks to Jonathan Cole for allowing me access to the Columbia University Library. Joanna Lewis Cole has given me more helpful advice and information than I can keep track of. And thanks to Sandy Meagher for many good conversations, help in researching children's books, and a lot of rides. A final thanks to my parents, Harry Mazer and Norma Fox Mazer, who are invisible presences in all of my books. —A.M.

The publisher wishes to thank Robert Kane of the New York City School Volunteer Program, Inc. for his encouragement and advice regarding many aspects of the publication of *America Street*.

For information, contact the publisher:
Persea Books, Inc.
853 Broadway
New York, New York 10003

Library of Congress Cataloging-in-Publication Data

American street : a multicultural anthology of stories / edited by Anne Mazer.
p. cm.
Summary: Fourteen stories by American authors from diverse racial and cultural backgrounds, including Duane Big Eagle, Nicholasa Mohr, Lensey Namioka, and Robert Cormier.
ISBN 0-89255-190-9 : $14.95.—ISBN 0-89255-191-7 : $4.95
1. Children's stories, American. [1. Short stories.] I. Mazer, Anne.
PZ5.A5145   1993
[Fic]—dc20

93-3465
CIP
AC

Designed by REM Studio, Inc.
Set in ITC Zapf International Light by Keystrokes, Lenox, Massachusetts
Printed on acid-free, recycled paper and bound by The Haddon Craftsmen,
Bloomsburg, Pennsylvania
Jacket and cover printed by Lynn Art, New York, New York

03 04 05 RRD 12 11 10

CONTENTS

INTRODUCTION

Welcome to *America Street*, an anthology of fourteen stories by some of our best American writers about the complex experience of growing up in our diverse society. It is the first of its kind for younger readers. And yet it is nothing more revolutionary than a reflection of the world around us. We have gathered stories about young people in cities and in rural areas across the United States. They are Native, Asian, Latino, European, African, Arab, and Jewish—some recently arrived from other countries, some born in the United States. All are finding their way, facing the realities of home, school, and friendship, and trying to make a place for themselves.

Like all fine fiction, the stories in *America Street* have the power to transform our understanding. They allow us to enter into another person's experience and to feel it as if it were our own. In Nicholasa Mohr's "The Wrong Lunch Line," Yvette, a Latina, finds that sharing a school Passover lunch with her best friend is more difficult than she expected. A Native American boy in "The Journey" by Duane Big Eagle travels from his home in Mexico to the American west—a journey that takes him from sickness to health, and from childhood to maturity. Toni Cade Bambara's "Raymond's Run" describes a young Black girl's radiant pride and determination as she trains for a neighborhood race. And the Chinese American protagonist in Lensey Namioka's hilarious "The All-American Slurp" finds that even something as ordinary as eating a stalk of celery can differ from one culture to another. Immediate, powerful, and superbly written, these stories are sure to evoke recognition and engage the sympathy of their readers.

America Street is a collection of some of the best in contemporary American fiction. It is also a meeting place of people and ideas, like our classrooms, our neighborhoods, and our country. In these pages it is our privilege to get to know many different people and to hear many different voices. In the best American tradition, they speak for themselves.

—ANNE MAZER

AMERICA STREET

THE JOURNEY

Duane Big Eagle

I had known the train all my life. Its wailing roar rushed through my dreams as through a tunnel and yet I had never even been on one. Now I was to take one on a two-thousand-kilometer journey halfway into a foreign country!

This particular adventure was my fault, if you can call being sick a fault. Mama says finding fault is only a way of clouding a problem and this problem was clouded enough. It began when I was thirteen. I still have tuberculosis scars on my lungs, but this illness was more than tuberculosis. The regular doctors were mystified by the fevers and delirium that accompanied a bad cough and nausea. After six months of treatment without improvement they gave up.

Papa carried me on his back as we left the doctor's office and began our walk to the barrio that was our home. Mama cried as she walked and Papa seemed weighted by more than the weight of my thinned-down frame. About halfway home Papa suddenly straightened up. I was having a dizzy spell and almost slipped off his back but he caught me with one hand and shouted, "Aunt Rosalie! What a fool I am! Aunt Rosalie Stands Tall!" Papa started to laugh and to dance around and around on the dirt path in the middle of a field.

"What do you mean?" cried Mama as she rushed around with her hands out, ready to catch me if I fell. From the look on her face, the real question in her mind was more like, Have you gone mad? "Listen, woman," said Papa, "there are some people who can cure diseases the medical doctors can't. Aunt Rosalie Stands Tall is a medicine woman of the Yaqui people and one of the best! She'll be able to cure Raoul! The only problem is she's married to an Indian in the United States. But that can't be helped, we'll just have to go there. Come on, we have plans to make and work to do!"

The planning began that day. We had very little money, but with what we had and could borrow from Papa's many friends there was just enough for a child's ticket to the little town in Oklahoma where Rosalie lived. I couldn't be left alone in a foreign country so Papa decided simply to walk. "I'll take the main highway north to the old Papago trails that go across the desert. They'll also take me across the border undetected. Then I'll head east and north to Oklahoma. It should be easy to catch occasional rides once I get to the U.S. When I arrive I'll send word for Raoul to start."

Papa left one fine spring morning, taking only a blanket, a few extra pairs of shoes, bow and arrows to catch food, and a flintstone for building fires. Secretly I believe he was happy to be travelling again. Travel had always been in his blood. As a young man, Papa got a job on a sailing ship and travelled all over the world. This must have been how he learned to speak English and also how he met Mama in the West Indies. Myself, I was still sixty kilometers from the town I was born in and even to imagine the journey I was about to take was more than my fevered brain could handle. But as Mama said, "You can do anything in the world if you take it little by little and one step at a time." This was the miraculous and trusting philosophy our family lived by, and I must admit it has usually worked.

Still, the day of departure found me filled with a dread that settled like lead in my feet. If I hadn't been so light-headed from the fevers, I'm sure I would have fallen over at any attempt to walk. Dressed in my best clothes which looked shabby the minute we got to the train station, Mama led me into the fourth-class carriage and found me a seat on a bench near the windows. Then she disappeared and came back a minute later with a thin young man with sallow skin and a drooping Zapata mustache. "This is your second cousin, Alejandro. He is a conductor on this train and will be with you till you get to Juarez; you must do whatever he says."

At that time, the conductors on trains in Mexico were required to stay with a train the entire length of its journey which perhaps accounted for Alejandro's appearance. He did little to inspire my confidence in him. In any case, he disappeared a second later and it was time for Mama to go too. Hurriedly, she reminded me that there was money in my coat to buy food from the women who came onto the train at every stop and that there was a silver bracelet sewn into the cuff of my pants to bribe the guards at the border. With one last tearful kiss and hug, she was gone and I was alone. The train started with a jerk which knocked me off my bench and I began my journey upside down in a heap on top of my crumpled cardboard suitcase. I didn't even get a chance to wave goodbye.

I soon got used to the jerking starts of the train, and unsmiling Alejandro turned out to be a guardian angel which was fortunate because my illness began to get worse as the journey went along. Many times I awoke to find Alejandro shuffling some young thief away from my meager possessions or buying me food at the last stop before a long stretch of desert. He would bring me things too, fresh peaches and apples and left-over bread and pastries from the first-class carriages where he worked. Once, in the middle of the desert he brought me a small ice-cold watermelon, the most refreshing thing I'd ever tasted—who knows where he got it?

To this day, I'm not sure exactly which of the things I saw through the window of the train were real and which were not. Some of them I know were not real. In my delirium, a half day's journey would pass in the blink of an eye. Often I noticed only large changes in the countryside, from plains to mountains to desert. Broad valleys remain clearly in my mind and there were many of these. Small scenes, too, remain—a family sitting down to dinner at a candle-lit table in a hut by a river. And a few more sinister ones—once between two pine trees I caught a glimpse of one man raising a large club to strike another man whose back was turned. I cried out but there was nothing to be done, the train was moving too fast on a downgrade and probably couldn't have been stopped. But then, did I really see them at all? My doubt was caused by the girl in the dark red dress.

I think I began to see her about halfway through the journey to Juarez. She was very beautiful, high cheekbones, long black hair and very dark skin. She was about my height and age or maybe a little older. Her eyes were very large and her mouth seemed to have a ready smile. The first time I saw her, at a small station near a lake, she smiled and waved as the train pulled away. Her sensuality embarrassed me and I didn't wave back. I regretted it immediately. But she was back again the next day at a station in the foothills of the mountains, this time dressed in the white blouse and skirt that the Huichol women wear.

She became almost a regular occurrence. Sometimes she was happy, sometimes serious and most of the time she was wearing the dark red dress. Often I would only see her in passing; she'd be working in a field and rise up to watch the train go by. Gradually, my condition grew worse. My coughing fits grew longer and I slept more so I began not to see the girl so much, but the last time I saw her really gave me a shock. The mountains of the Sierra Madre Oriental range are very rugged and are cut in places by deep gorges called barrancas. The train was in one of these gorges on a ledge above the river and was about to go around a bend. For some reason, I looked back the way we had come and there, imbedded in the mountain with her eyes closed, was the face of the girl, thirty feet high! For the first time, I noticed the small crescent-shaped scar in the middle of her lower lip.

The vision, or whatever it was, quickly disappeared as the train rounded the curve. I sank back on to the bench with a pounding heart and closed my eyes. I must have slept or perhaps I fell into a coma because I remember very little of the last part of the trip. I awoke once while Alejandro was carrying me across the border and delivering me to a friend of his on the train to Dallas. How I got from Dallas to Oklahoma I may never know because I remember nothing. But it happened. And finally, I awoke for a minute in my father's arms as he carried me off the train.

Then, there was a sharp pain in the center of my chest. And a pounding. Rhythmic pounding. A woman's voice began to sing in a very high pitch. My eyes opened of themselves. At first I couldn't make it out, arched crossing lines, flickering shadows. I was in the center of an oval-shaped lodge built of bent willow limbs covered with skins and lit by a small fire. A tall woman came into view; she was singing and dancing back and forth. Somehow I knew this was Rosalie Stands Tall, the medicine woman. The pain hit me again and I wanted to get away but hands held me still.

Papa's voice said in my ear, "She is calling her spirit helpers, you must try and sit up." I was sitting up facing the door of the lodge. There was a lizard there and he spoke in an old man's voice, words I couldn't understand. Rosalie sang again and there was a small hawk there. The pain rose up higher in my chest. There was a coyote in the door and his words were tinged with mocking laughter. The pain rose into my throat. There was a small brown bear in the door, his fur blew back and forth in the wind. The pain rose into the back of my mouth. I felt I needed to cough. Rosalie put two porcupine quills together and bound them with leather to make a pair of tweezers. She held my lips closed with them, painfully tight. A pair of wings beat against the top of the lodge. I needed badly to cough. There was something hot in my mouth, it was sharp, it was hurting my mouth, it needed to come out! IT WAS OUT!

I awoke in bed in a small room lit by a coal-oil lamp. There was a young woman with her back to me preparing food by the side of the bed. She had very long black hair. She put the tray down on the table beside the bed. As she turned to leave the room, I saw a small crescent-shaped scar in the middle of her lower lip. I started to call her back but there was no need. I knew who she was. An immense peacefulness settled over me. It was warm in the bed. Papa sat on the other side of the bed. He seemed very happy when I turned and looked at him. He said softly, "Raoul, you have changed completely. You're not anymore the young boy I left in Mazatlan." I wanted to tell him everything! There was so much to say! But all I could get out was, "Yes, I know, Papa, I've come on a journey out of childhood." And then I went to sleep again.

RAYMOND'S RUN

Toni Cade Bambara

I don't have much work to do around the house like some girls. My mother does that. And I don't have to earn my pocket money by hustling; George runs errands for the big boys and sells Christmas cards. And anything else that's got to get done, my father does. All I have to do in life is mind my brother Raymond, which is enough.

Sometimes I slip and say my little brother Raymond. But as any fool can see he's much bigger and he's older too. But a lot of people call him my little brother cause he needs looking after cause he's not quite right. And a lot of smart mouths got lots to say about that too, especially when George was minding him. But now, if anybody has anything to say to Raymond, anything to say about his big head, they have to come by me. And I don't play the dozens or believe in standing around with somebody in my face doing a lot of talking. I much rather just knock you down and take my chances even if I am a little girl with skinny arms and a squeaky voice, which is how I got the name Squeaky. And if things get too rough, I run. And as anybody can tell you, I'm the fastest thing on two feet.

There is no track meet that I don't win the first place medal. I used to win the twenty-yard dash when I was a little kid in kindergarten. Nowadays, it's the fifty-yard dash. And tomorrow I'm subject to run the quarter-meter relay all by myself and come in first, second, and third. The big kids call me Mercury cause I'm the swiftest thing in the neighborhood. Everybody knows that—except two people who know better, my father and me. He can beat me to Amsterdam Avenue with me having a two fire-hydrant headstart and him running with his hands in his pockets and whistling. But that's private information. Cause you can imagine some thirty-five-year-old man stuffing himself into PAL shorts to race little kids? So as far as everyone's concerned, I'm the fastest and that goes for Gretchen, too, who has put out the tale that she is going to win the first-place medal this year. Ridiculous. In the second place, she's got short legs. In the third place, she's got freckles. In the first place, no one can beat me and that's all there is to it.

I'm standing on the corner admiring the weather and about to take a stroll down Broadway so I can practice my breathing exercises, and I've got Raymond walking on the inside close to the buildings, cause he's subject to fits of fantasy and starts thinking he's a circus performer and that the curb is a tightrope strung high in the air. And sometimes after a rain he likes to step down off his tightrope right into the gutter and slosh around getting his shoes and cuffs wet. Then I get hit when I get home. Or sometimes if you don't watch him he'll dash across traffic to the island in the middle of Broadway and give the pigeons a fit. Then I have to go behind him apologizing to all the old people sitting around trying to get some sun and getting all upset with the pigeons fluttering around them, scattering their news-papers and upsetting the waxpaper lunches in their laps. So I keep Raymond on the inside of me, and he plays like he's driving a stage coach which is O.K. by me so long as he doesn't run me over or interrupt my breathing exercises, which I have to do on account of I'm serious about my running, and I don't care who knows it.

Now some people like to act like things come easy to them, won't let on that they practice. Not me. I'll high-prance down 34th Street like a rodeo pony to keep my knees strong even if it does get my mother uptight so that she walks ahead like she's not with me, don't know me, is all by herself on a shopping trip, and I am somebody else's crazy child. Now you take Cynthia Procter for instance. She's just the opposite. If there's a test tomorrow, she'll say something like, "Oh, I guess I'll play handball this afternoon and watch television tonight," just to let you know she ain't thinking about the test. Or like last week when she won the spelling bee for the millionth time, "A good thing you got 'receive,' Squeaky, cause I would have got it wrong. I completely forgot about the spelling bee." And she'll clutch the lace on her blouse like it was a narrow escape. Oh, brother. But of course when I pass her house on my early morning trots around the block, she is practicing the scales on the piano over and over and over and over. Then in music class she always lets herself get bumped around so she falls accidently on purpose onto the piano stool and is so surprised to find herself sitting there that she decides just for fun to try out the ole keys. And what do you know—Chopin's waltzes just spring out of her fingertips and she's the most surprised thing in the world. A regular prodigy. I could kill people like that. I stay up all night studying the words for the spelling bee. And you can see me any time of day practicing running. I never walk if I can trot, and shame on Raymond if he can't keep up. But of course he does, cause if he hangs back someone's liable to walk up to him and get smart, or take his allowance from him, or ask him where he got that great big pumpkin head. People are so stupid sometimes.

So I'm strolling down Broadway breathing out and breathing in on counts of seven, which is my lucky number, and here comes Gretchen and her sidekicks: Mary Louise, who used to be a friend of mine when she first moved to Harlem from Baltimore and got beat up by everybody till I took up for her on account of her mother and my mother used to sing in the same choir when they were young girls, but people ain't grateful, so now she hangs out with the new girl Gretchen and talks about me like a dog; and Rosie, who is as fat as I am skinny and has a big mouth where Raymond is concerned and is too stupid to know that there is not a big deal of difference between herself and Raymond and that she can't afford to throw stones. So they are steady coming up Broadway and I see right away that it's going to be one of those Dodge City scenes cause the street ain't that big and they're close to the buildings just as we are. First I think I'll step into the candy store and look over the new comics and let them pass. But that's chicken and I've got a reputation to consider. So then I think I'll just walk straight on through them or even over them if necessary. But as they get to me, they slow down. I'm ready to fight, cause like I said I don't feature a whole lot of chit-chat, I much prefer to just knock you down right from the jump and save everybody a lotta precious time.

"You signing up for the May Day races?" smiles Mary Louise, only it's not a smile at all. A dumb question like that doesn't deserve an answer. Besides, there's just me and Gretchen standing there really, so no use wasting my breath talking to shadows.

"I don't think you're going to win this time," says Rosie, trying to signify with her hands on her hips all salty, completely forgetting that I have whupped her behind many times for less salt than that.

"I always win cause I'm the best," I say straight at Gretchen who is, as far as I'm concerned, the only one talking in this ventriloquist-dummy routine. Gretchen smiles, but it's not a smile, and I'm thinking that girls never really smile at each other because they don't know how and don't want to know how and there's probably no one to teach us how, cause grown-up girls don't know either. Then they all look at Raymond who has just brought his mule team to a standstill. And they're about to see what trouble they can get into through him.

"What grade you in now, Raymond?"

"You got anything to say to my brother, you say it to me, Mary Louise Williams of Raggedy Town, Baltimore."

"What are you, his mother?" sasses Rosie.

"That's right, Fatso. And the next word out of anybody and I'll be *their* mother too." So they just stand there and Gretchen shifts from one leg to the other and so do they. Then Gretchen puts her hands on her hips and is about to say something with her freckle-face self but doesn't. Then she walks around me looking me up and down but keeps walking up Broadway, and her sidekicks follow her. So me and Raymond smile at each other and he says, "Gidyap" to his team and I continue with my breathing exercises, strolling down Broadway toward the ice man on 145th with not a care in the world cause I am Miss Quicksilver herself.

I take my time getting to the park on May Day because the track meet is the last thing on the program. The biggest thing on the program is the May Pole dancing, which I can do without, thank you, even if my mother thinks it's a shame I don't take part and act like a girl for a change. You'd think my mother'd be grateful not to have to make me a white organdy dress with a big satin sash and buy me new white baby-doll shoes that can't be taken out of the box till the big day. You'd think she'd be glad her daughter ain't out there prancing around a May Pole getting the new clothes all dirty and sweaty and trying to act like a fairy or a flower or whatever you're supposed to be when you should be trying to be yourself, whatever that is, which is, as far as I am concerned, a poor Black girl who really can't afford to buy shoes and a new dress you only wear once a lifetime cause it won't fit next year.

I was once a strawberry in a Hansel and Gretel pageant when I was in nursery school and didn't have no better sense than to dance on tiptoe with my arms in a circle over my head doing umbrella steps and being a perfect fool just so my mother and father could come dressed up and clap. You'd think they'd know better than to encourage that kind of nonsense. I am not a strawberry. I do not dance on my toes. I run. That is what I am all about. So I always come late to the May Day program, just in time to get my number pinned on and lay in the grass till they announce the fifty-yard dash.

I put Raymond in the little swings, which is a tight squeeze this year and will be impossible next year. Then I look around for Mr. Pearson, who pins the numbers on. I'm really looking for Gretchen if you want to know the truth, but she's not around. The park is jam-packed. Parents in hats and corsages and breast-pocket handkerchiefs peeking up. Kids in white dresses and light-blue suits. The parkees unfolding chairs and chasing the rowdy kids from Lenox as if they had no right to be there. The big guys with their caps on backwards, leaning against the fence swirling the basketballs on the tips of their fingers, waiting for all these crazy people to clear out the park so they can play. Most of the kids in my class are carrying bass drums and glockenspiels and flutes. You'd think they'd put in a few bongos or something for real like that.

Then here comes Mr. Pearson with his clipboard and his cards and pencils and whistles and safety pins and fifty million other things he's always dropping all over the place with his clumsy self. He sticks out in a crowd because he's on stilts. We used to call him Jack and the Beanstalk to get him mad. But I'm the only one that can outrun him and get away, and I'm too grown for that silliness now.

"Well, Squeaky," he says, checking my name off the list and handing me number seven and two pins. And I'm thinking he's got no right to call me Squeaky, if I can't call him Beanstalk.

"Hazel Elizabeth Deborah Parker," I correct him and tell him to write it down on his board.

"Well, Hazel Elizabeth Deborah Parker, going to give someone else a break this year?" I squint at him real hard to see if he is seriously thinking I should lose the race on purpose just to give someone else a break. "Only six girls running this time," he continues, shaking his head sadly like it's my fault all of New York didn't turn out in sneakers. "That new girl should give you a run for your money." He looks around the park for Gretchen like a periscope in a submarine movie. "Wouldn't it be a nice gesture if you were . . . to ahhh . . ."

I give him such a look he couldn't finish putting that idea into words. Grownups got a lot of nerve sometimes. I pin number seven to myself and stomp away, I'm so burnt. And I go straight for the track and stretch out on the grass while the band winds up with "Oh, the Monkey Wrapped his Tail Around the Flag Pole," which my teacher calls by some other name. The man on the loudspeaker is calling

everyone over to the track and I'm on my back looking at
the sky, trying to pretend I'm in the country, but I can't,
because even grass in the city feels hard as sidewalk, and
there's just no pretending you are anywhere but in a "concrete jungle" as my grandfather says.

The twenty-yard dash takes all of two minutes cause
most of the little kids don't know no better than to run off
the track or run the wrong way or run smack into the fence
and fall down and cry. One little kid, though, has got the
good sense to run straight for the white ribbon up ahead
so he wins. Then the second-graders line up for the thirty-
yard dash and I don't even bother to turn my head to watch
cause Raphael Perez always wins. He wins before he even
begins by psyching the runners, telling them they're going
to trip on their shoelaces and fall on their faces or lose their
shorts or something, which he doesn't really have to do
since he is very fast, almost as fast as I am. After that is
the forty-yard dash which I use to run when I was in first
grade. Raymond is hollering from the swings cause he knows
I'm about to do my thing cause the man on the loudspeaker
has just announced the fifty-yard dash, although he might
just as well be giving a recipe for angel food cake cause you
can hardly make out what he's sayin for the static. I get up
and slip off my sweat pants and then I see Gretchen standing
at the starting line, kicking her legs out like a pro. Then as
I get into place I see that ole Raymond is on line on the
other side of the fence, bending down with his fingers on
the ground just like he knew what he was doing. I was
going to yell at him but then I didn't. It burns up your
energy to holler.

Every time, just before I take off in a race, I always feel like I'm in a dream, the kind of dream you have when you're sick with fever and feel all hot and weightless. I dream I'm flying over a sandy beach in the early morning sun, kissing the leaves of the trees as I fly by. And there's always the smell of apples, just like in the country when I was little and used to think I was a choo-choo train, running through the fields of corn and chugging up the hill to the orchard. And all the time I'm dreaming this, I get lighter and lighter until I'm flying over the beach again, getting blown through the sky like a feather that weighs nothing at all. But once I spread my fingers in the dirt and crouch over the Get on Your Mark, the dream goes and I am solid again and am telling myself, Squeaky you must win, you must win, you are the fastest thing in the world, you can even beat your father up Amsterdam if you really try. And then I feel my weight coming back just behind my knees then down to my feet then into the earth and the pistol shot explodes in my blood and I am off and weightless again, flying past the other runners, my arms pumping up and down and the whole world is quiet except for the crunch as I zoom over the gravel in the track. I glance to my left and there is no one. To the right, a blurred Gretchen, who's got her chin jutting out as if it would win the race all by itself. And on the other side of the fence is Raymond with his arms down to his side and the palms tucked up behind him, running in his very own style, and it's the first time I ever saw that and I almost stop to watch my brother Raymond on his first run. But the white ribbon is bouncing toward me and I tear past it, racing into the distance till

my feet with a mind of their own start digging up footfuls
of dirt and brake me short. Then all the kids standing on
the side pile on me, banging me on the back and slapping
my head with their May Day programs, for I have won
again and everybody on 151st Street can walk tall for another
year.

"In first place..." the man on the loudspeaker is clear
as a bell now. But then he pauses and the loudspeaker starts
to whine. Then static. And I lean down to catch my breath
and here comes Gretchen walking back, for she's overshot
the finish line too, huffing and puffing with her hands on
her hips taking it slow, breathing in steady time like a real
pro and I sort of like her a little for the first time. "In first
place..." and then three or four voices get all mixed up on
the loudspeaker and I dig my sneaker into the grass and
stare at Gretchen who's staring back, we both wondering
just who did win. I can hear old Beanstalk arguing with
the man on the loudspeaker and then a few others running
their mouths about what the stopwatches say. Then I hear
Raymond yanking at the fence to call me and I wave to
shush him, but he keeps rattling the fence like a gorilla in
a cage like in them gorilla movies, but then like a dancer
or something he starts climbing up nice and easy but very
fast. And it occurs to me, watching how smoothly he climbs
hand over hand and remembering how he looked running
with his arms down to his side and with the wind pulling
his mouth back and his teeth showing and all, it occurred
to me that Raymond would make a very fine runner. Doesn't
he always keep up with me on my trots? And he surely
knows how to breathe in counts of seven cause he's always

doing it at the dinner table, which drives my brother George up the wall. And I'm smiling to beat the band cause if I've lost this race, or if me and Gretchen tied, or even if I've won, I can always retire as a runner and begin a whole new career as a coach with Raymond as my champion. After all, with a little more study I can beat Cynthia and her phony self at the spelling bee. And if I bugged my mother, I could get piano lessons and become a star. And I have a big rep as the baddest thing around. And I've got a roomful of ribbons and medals and awards. But what has Raymond got to call his own?

So I stand there with my new plans, laughing out loud by this time as Raymond jumps down from the fence and runs over with his teeth showing and his arms down to the side, which no one before him has quite mastered as a running style. And by the time he comes over I'm jumping up and down so glad to see him—my brother Raymond, a great runner in the family tradition. But of course everyone thinks I'm jumping up and down because the men on the loudspeaker have finally gotten themselves together and compared notes and are announcing "In first place—Miss Hazel Elizabeth Deborah Parker." (Dig that.) "In second place—Miss Gretchen P. Lewis." And I look over at Gretchen wondering what the "P" stands for. And I smile. Cause she's good, no doubt about it. Maybe she'd like to help me coach Raymond; she obviously is serious about running, as any fool can see. And she nods to congratulate me and then she smiles. And I smile. We stand there with this big smile of respect between us. It's about as real a smile as girls can do for each other, considering we don't practice real smiling every day, you know, cause maybe we too busy being flowers or fairies or strawberries instead of something honest and worthy of respect ... you know ... like being people.

THE CIRCUIT

Francisco Jiménez

It was that time of year again. Ito, the strawberry share-cropper, did not smile. It was natural. The peak of the strawberry season was over and the last few days the workers, most of them braceros, were not picking as many boxes as they had during the months of June and July.

As the last days of August disappeared, so did the number of braceros. Sunday, only one—the best picker—came to work. I liked him. Sometimes we talked during our half-hour lunch break. That is how I found out he was from Jalisco, the same state in Mexico my family was from. That Sunday was the last time I saw him.

When the sun had tired and sunk behind the mountains, Ito signaled us that it was time to go home. "Ya esora," he yelled in his broken Spanish. Those were the words I waited for twelve hours a day, every day, seven days a week, week after week. And the thought of not hearing them again saddened me.

As we drove home Papá did not say a word. With both hands on the wheel, he stared at the dirt road. My older brother, Roberto, was also silent. He leaned his head back and closed his eyes. Once in a while he cleared from his throat the dust that blew in from outside.

Yes, it was that time of year. When I opened the front door to the shack, I stopped. Everything we owned was neatly packed in cardboard boxes. Suddenly I felt even more the weight of hours, days, weeks, and months of work. I sat down on a box. The thought of having to move to Fresno and knowing what was in store for me there brought tears to my eyes.

That night I could not sleep. I lay in bed thinking about how much I hated this move.

A little before five o'clock in the morning, Papá woke everyone up. A few minutes later, the yelling and screaming of my little brothers and sisters, for whom the move was a great adventure, broke the silence of dawn. Shortly, the barking of the dogs accompanied them.

While we packed the breakfast dishes, Papá went outside to start the "Carcanchita." That was the name Papá gave his old '38 black Plymouth. He bought it in a used-car lot in Santa Rosa in the winter of 1949. Papá was very proud of his little jalopy. He had a right to be proud of it. He spent a lot of time looking at other cars before buying this one.

When he finally chose the "Carcanchita," he checked it thoroughly before driving it out of the car lot. He examined every inch of the car. He listened to the motor, tilting his head from side to side like a parrot, trying to detect any noises that spelled car trouble. After being satisfied with the looks and sounds of the car, Papá then insisted on knowing who the original owner was. He never did find out from the car salesman, but he bought the car anyway. Papá figured the original owner must have been an important man because behind the rear seat of the car he found a blue necktie.

Papá parked the car out in front and left the motor running. "Listo," he yelled. Without saying a word, Roberto and I began to carry the boxes out to the car. Roberto carried the two big boxes and I carried the two smaller ones. Papá then threw the mattress on top of the car roof and tied it with ropes to the front and rear bumpers.

Everything was packed except Mamá's pot. It was an old large galvanized pot she had picked up at an army surplus store in Santa María the year I was born. The pot had many dents and nicks, and the more dents and nicks it acquired the more Mamá liked it. "Mi olla," she used to say proudly.

I held the front door open as Mamá carefully carried out her pot by both handles, making sure not to spill the cooked beans. When she got to the car, Papá reached out to help her with it. Roberto opened the rear car door and Papá gently placed it on the floor behind the front seat. All of us then climbed in. Papá sighed, wiped the sweat off his forehead with his sleeve, and said wearily: "Es todo."

As we drove away, I felt a lump in my throat. I turned around and looked at our little shack for the last time.

At sunset we drove into a labor camp near Fresno. Since Papá did not speak English, Mamá asked the camp foreman if he needed any more workers. "We don't need no more," said the foreman, scratching his head. "Check with Sullivan down the road. Can't miss him. He lives in a big white house with a fence around it."

When we got there, Mamá walked up to the house. She went through a white gate, past a row of rose bushes, up the stairs to the front door. She rang the doorbell. The porch light went on and a tall husky man came out. They exchanged a few words. After the man went in, Mamá clasped her hands and hurried back to the car. "We have work! Mr. Sullivan said we can stay there the whole season," she said, gasping and pointing to an old garage near the stables.

The garage was worn out by the years. It had no windows. The walls, eaten by termites, strained to support the roof full of holes. The dirt floor, populated by earth worms, looked like a gray road map.

That night, by the light of a kerosene lamp, we unpacked and cleaned our new home. Roberto swept away the loose dirt, leaving the hard ground. Papá plugged the holes in the walls with old newspapers and tin can tops. Mamá fed my little brothers and sisters. Papá and Roberto then brought in the mattress and placed it on the far corner of the garage. "Mamá, you and the little ones sleep on the mattress. Robert, Panchito, and I will sleep outside under the trees," Papá said.

Early next morning Mr. Sullivan showed us where his crop was, and after breakfast, Papá, Roberto, and I headed for the vineyard to pick.

Around nine o'clock the temperature had risen to almost one hundred degrees. I was completely soaked in sweat and my mouth felt as if I had been chewing on a handkerchief. I walked over to the end of the row, picked up the jug of water we had brought, and began drinking. "Don't drink too much; you'll get sick," Roberto shouted. No sooner had he said that than I felt sick to my stomach. I dropped to my knees and let the jug roll off my hands. I remained motionless with my eyes glued on the hot sandy ground. All I could hear was the drone of insects. Slowly I began to recover. I poured water over my face and neck and watched the dirty water run down my arms to the ground.

I still felt a little dizzy when we took a break to eat lunch. It was past two o'clock and we sat underneath a large walnut tree that was on the side of the road. While we ate, Papá jotted down the number of boxes we had picked. Roberto drew designs on the ground with a stick. Suddenly I noticed Papá's face turn pale as he looked down the road. "Here comes the school bus," he whispered loudly in alarm. Instinctively, Roberto and I ran and hid in the vineyards. We did not want to get in trouble for not going to school. The neatly dressed boys about my age got off. They carried books under their arms. After they crossed the street, the bus drove away. Roberto and I came out from hiding and joined Papá. "Tienen que tener cuidado," he warned us.

After lunch we went back to work. The sun kept beating

down. The buzzing insects, the wet sweat, and the hot dry dust made the afternoon seem to last forever. Finally the mountains around the valley reached out and swallowed the sun. Within an hour it was too dark to continue picking. The vines blanketed the grapes, making it difficult to see the bunches. "Vámonos," said Papá, signaling to us that it was time to quit work. Papá then took out a pencil and began to figure out how much we had earned our first day. He wrote down numbers, crossed some out, wrote down some more. "Quince," he murmured.

When we arrived home, we took a cold shower underneath a waterhose. We then sat down to eat dinner around some wooden crates that served as a table. Mamá had cooked a special meal for us. We had rice and tortillas with "carne con chile," my favorite dish.

The next morning I could hardly move. My body ached all over. I felt little control over my arms and legs. This feeling went on every morning for days until my muscles finally got used to the work.

It was Monday, the first week of November. The grape season was over and I could now go to school. I woke up early that morning and lay in bed, looking at the stars and savoring the thought of not going to work and of starting sixth grade for the first time that year. Since I could not sleep, I decided to get up and join Papá and Roberto at breakfast. I sat at the table across from Roberto, but I kept my head down. I did not want to look up and face him. I knew he was sad. He was not going to school today. He was not going tomorrow, or next week, or next month. He would not go until the cotton season was over, and that was sometime in February. I rubbed my hands together and watched the dry, acid stained skin fall to the floor in little rolls.

When Papá and Roberto left for work, I felt relief. I walked to the top of a small grade next to the shack and watched the "Carcanchita" disappear in the distance in a cloud of dust.

Two hours later, around eight o'clock, I stood by the side of the road waiting for school bus number twenty. When it arrived I climbed in. Everyone was busy either talking or yelling. I sat in an empty seat in the back.

When the bus stopped in front of the school, I felt very nervous. I looked out the bus window and saw boys and girls carrying books under their arms. I put my hands in my pant pockets and walked to the principal's office. When I entered I heard a woman's voice say: "May I help you?" I was startled. I had not heard English for months. For a few seconds I remained speechless. I looked at the lady who waited for an answer. My first instinct was to answer her in Spanish, but I held back. Finally, after struggling for English words, I managed to tell her that I wanted to enroll in the sixth grade. After answering many questions, I was led to the classroom.

Mr. Lema, the sixth grade teacher, greeted me and assigned me a desk. He then introduced me to the class. I was so nervous and scared at that moment when everyone's eyes were on me that I wished I were with Papá and Roberto picking cotton. After taking roll, Mr. Lema gave the class the assignment for the first hour. "The first thing we have to do this morning is finish reading the story we began yesterday," he said enthusiastically. He walked up to me, handed me an English book, and asked me to read. "We are on page 125," he said politely. When I heard this, I felt my blood rush to my head; I felt dizzy. "Would you like to read?" he asked hesitantly. I opened the book to page 125. My mouth was dry. My eyes began to water. I could not begin. "You can read later," Mr. Lema said understandingly.

For the rest of the reading period I kept getting angrier and angrier with myself. I should have read, I thought to myself.

During recess I went into the restroom and opened my English book to page 125. I began to read in a low voice, pretending I was in class. There were many words I did not know. I closed the book and headed back to the class-room.

Mr. Lema was sitting at his desk correcting papers. When I entered he looked up at me and smiled. I felt better. I walked up to him and asked if he could help me with the new words. "Gladly," he said.

The rest of the month I spent my lunch hours working on English with Mr. Lema, my best friend at school.

One Friday during lunch hour Mr. Lema asked me to take a walk with him to the music room. "Do you like music?" he asked me as we entered the building.

"Yes, I like corridos," I answered. He then picked up a trumpet, blew on it and handed it to me. The sound gave me goose bumps. I knew that sound. I had heard it in many corridos. "How would you like to learn how to play it?" he asked. He must have read my face because before I could answer, he added: "I'll teach you how to play it during our lunch hours."

That day I could hardly wait to get home to tell Papá and Mamá the great news. As I got off the bus, my little brothers and sisters ran up to meet me. They were yelling and screaming. I thought they were happy to see me, but when I opened the door to our shack, I saw that everything we owned was neatly packed in cardboard boxes.

THE WRONG LUNCH LINE

Nicholasa Mohr

Early Spring 1946

The morning dragged on for Yvette and Mildred. They were anxiously waiting for the bell to ring. Last Thursday the school had announced that free Passover lunches would be provided for the Jewish children during this week. Yvette ate the free lunch provided by the school and Mildred brought her lunch from home in a brown paper bag. Because of school rules, free-lunch children and bag-lunch children could not sit in the same section, and the two girls always ate separately. This week, however, they had planned to eat together.

Finally the bell sounded and all the children left the classroom for lunch. As they had already planned, Yvette and Mildred went right up to the line where the Jewish children were filing up for lunch-trays. I hope no one asks me nothing, Yvette said to herself. They stood close to each other and held hands. Every once in a while one would squeeze the other's hand in a gesture of reassurance, and they would giggle softly.

The two girls lived just a few houses away from one another. Yvette lived on the top floor of a tenement, in a four-room apartment which she shared with her parents, grandmother, three older sisters, two younger brothers, and baby sister. Mildred was an only child. She lived with her parents in the three small rooms in back of the candy store they owned.

During this school year, the two girls had become good friends. Every day after public school, Mildred went to a Hebrew school. Yvette went to catechism twice a week, preparing for her First Communion and Confirmation. Most evenings after supper, they played together in front of the candy store. Yvette was a frequent visitor in Mildred's apartment. They listened to their favorite radio programs together. Yvette looked forward to the Hershey's chocolate bar that Mr. Fox, Mildred's father, would give her.

The two girls waited patiently on the lunch line as they slowly moved along toward the food counter. Yvette was delighted when she saw what was placed on the trays: a hard-boiled egg, a bowl of soup that looked like vegetable, a large piece of cracker, milk, and an apple. She stretched over to see what the regular free lunch was, and it was the usual: a bowl of watery stew, two slices of dark bread, milk, and cooked prunes in a thick syrup. She was really glad to be standing with Mildred.

"Hey Yvette!" She heard someone call her name. It was Elba Cruz, one of her classmates. "What's happening? Why are you standing there?"

"I'm having lunch with Mildred today," she answered, and looked at Mildred, who nodded.

"Oh yeah?" Elba said. "Why are they getting a different lunch from us?"

"It's their special holiday and they gotta eat that special food, that's all," Yvette answered.

"But why?" persisted Elba.

"Else it's a sin, that's why. Just like we can't have no meat on Friday," Yvette said.

"A sin. . . . Why—why is it a sin?" This time, she looked at Mildred.

"It's a special lunch for Passover," Mildred said.

"Passover? What is that?" asked Elba.

"It's a Jewish holiday. Like you got Easter, so we have Passover. We can't eat no bread."

"Oh. . . ."

"You better get in your line before the teacher comes," Yvette said quickly.

"You're here!" said Elba.

"I'm only here because Mildred invited me," Yvette answered. Elba shrugged her shoulders and walked away.

"They gonna kick you outta there. . . . I bet you are not supposed to be on that line," she called back to Yvette.

"Dumbbell!" Yvette answered. She turned to Mildred and asked, "Why can't you eat bread, Mildred?"

"We just can't. We are only supposed to eat matzo. What you see there." Mildred pointed to the large cracker on the tray.

"Oh," said Yvette. "Do you have to eat an egg too?"

"No . . . but you can't have no meat, because you can't have meat and milk together . . . like at the same time."

"Why?"

"Because it's against our religion. Besides, it's very bad. It's not supposed to be good for you."

"It's not?" asked Yvette.

"No," Mildred said. "You might get sick. You see, you are better off waiting like a few hours until you digest your food, and then you can have meat or the milk. But not together."

"Wow," said Yvette. "You know, I have meat and milk together all the time. I wonder if my mother knows it's not good for you."

By this time the girls were at the counter. Mildred took one tray and Yvette quickly took another.

"I hope no one notices me," Yvette whispered to Mildred. As the two girls walked toward a long lunch table, they heard giggling, and Yvette saw Elba and some of the kids she usually ate lunch with pointing and laughing at her. Stupids, thought Yvette, ignoring them and following Mildred. The two girls sat down with the special lunch group.

Yvette whispered to Mildred, "This looks good!" and started to crack the eggshell.

Yvette felt Mildred's elbow digging in her side. "Watch out!" Mildred said.

"What is going on here?" It was the voice of one of the teachers who monitored them during lunch. Yvette looked up and saw the teacher coming toward her.

"You! You there!" the teacher said, pointing to Yvette. "What are you doing over there?" Yvette looked at the woman and was unable to speak.

"What are you doing over there?" she repeated.

"I went to get some lunch," Yvette said softly.

"What? Speak up! I can't hear you."

"I said . . . I went to get some lunch," she said a little louder.

"Are you entitled to a free lunch?"

"Yes."

"Well . . . and are you Jewish?"

Yvette stared at her and she could feel her face getting hot and flushed.

"I asked you a question. Are you Jewish?" Another teacher Yvette knew came over and the lunchroom became quiet. Everyone was looking at Yvette, waiting to hear what was said. She turned to look at Mildred, who looked just as frightened as she felt. Please don't let me cry, thought Yvette.

"What's the trouble?" asked the other teacher.

"This child," the woman pointed to Yvette, "is eating lunch here with the Jewish children, and I don't think she's Jewish. She doesn't—I've seen her before; she gets free lunch, all right. But she looks like one of the—" Hesitating, the woman went on, "She looks Spanish."

"I'm sure she's not Jewish," said the other teacher.

"All right now," said the first teacher, "what are you doing here? Are you Spanish?"

"Yes."

"Why did you come over here and get in that line? You went on the wrong lunch line!"

Yvette looked down at the tray in front of her.

"Get up and come with me. Right now!" Getting up, she dared not look around her. She felt her face was going to burn up. Some of the children were laughing; she could hear the suppressed giggles and an occasional "Ooooh." As she started to walk behind the teacher, she heard her say, "Go back and bring that tray." Yvette felt slightly weak at the knees but managed to turn around, and going back to the table, she returned the tray to the counter. A kitchen worker smiled nonchalantly and removed the tray full of food.

"Come on over to Mrs. Ralston's office," the teacher said, and gestured to Yvette that she walk in front of her this time.

Inside the vice-principal's office, Yvette stood, not daring to look at Mrs. Rachel Ralston while she spoke.

"You have no right to take someone else's place." Mrs. Ralston continued to speak in an even-tempered, almost pleasant voice. "This time we'll let it go, but next time we will notify your parents and you won't get off so easily. You have to learn, Yvette, right from wrong. Don't go where you don't belong. . . ."

Yvette left the office and heard the bell. Lunchtime was over.

Yvette and Mildred met after school in the street. It was late in the afternoon. Yvette was returning from the corner grocery with a food package, and Mildred was coming home from Hebrew school.

"How was Hebrew school?" asked Yvette.

"Okay." Mildred smiled and nodded. "Are you coming over tonight to listen to the radio? 'Mr. Keene, Tracer of Lost Persons' is on."

"Okay," said Yvette. "I gotta bring this up and eat. Then I'll come by."

Yvette finished supper and was given permission to visit her friend.

"Boy, that was a good program, wasn't it, Mildred?" Yvette ate her candy with delight.

Mildred nodded and looked at Yvette, not speaking. There was a long moment of silence. They wanted to talk about it, but it was as if this afternoon's incident could not be mentioned. Somehow each girl was afraid of disturbing that feeling of closeness they felt for one another. And yet when their eyes met they looked away with an embarrassed smile.

"I wonder what's on the radio next," Yvette said, breaking the silence.

"Nothing good for another half hour," Mildred answered. Impulsively, she asked quickly, "Yvette, you wanna have some matzo? We got some for the holidays."

"Is that the cracker they gave you this afternoon?"

"Yeah. We can have some."

"All right." Yvette smiled.

Mildred left the room and returned holding a large square cracker. Breaking off a piece, she handed it to Yvette.

"It don't taste like much, does it?" said Yvette.

"Only if you put something good on it," Mildred agreed, smiling.

"Boy, that Mrs. Ralston sure is dumb," Yvette said, giggling. They looked at each other and began to laugh loudly.

"Old dumb Mrs. Ralston," said Mildred, laughing convulsively. "She's scre . . . screwy."

"Yeah," Yvette said, laughing so hard tears began to roll down her cheeks. "Dop . . . dopey . . . M . . . Mi . . . Mrs. Ra . . . Ral . . . ston. . . ."

THE LOUDEST VOICE

Grace Paley

There is a certain place where dumb-waiters boom, doors slam, dishes crash; every window is a mother's mouth bidding the street shut up, go skate somewhere else, come home. My voice is the loudest.

There, my own mother is still as full of breathing as me and the grocer stands up to speak to her. "Mrs. Abramowitz," he says, "people should not be afraid of their children."

"Ah, Mr. Bialik," my mother replies, "if you say to her or her father 'Ssh,' they say, 'In the grave it will be quiet.'"

"From Coney Island to the cemetery," says my papa. "It's the same subway; it's the same fare."

I am right next to the pickle barrel. My pinky is making tiny whirlpools in the brine. I stop a moment to announce: "Campbell's Tomato Soup. Campbell's Vegetable Beef Soup. Campbell's S-c-otch Broth . . ."

"Be quiet," the grocer says, "the labels are coming off."

"Please, Shirley, be a little quiet," my mother begs me.

In that place the whole street groans: Be quiet! Be quiet! but steals from the happy chorus of my inside self not a tittle or a jot.

There, too, but just around the corner, is a red brick building that has been old for many years. Every morning the children stand before it in double lines which must be straight. They are not insulted. They are waiting anyway.

I am usually among them. I am, in fact, the first, since I begin with "A."

One cold morning the monitor tapped me on the shoulder. "Go to Room 409, Shirley Abramowitz," he said. I did as I was told. I went in a hurry up a down staircase to Room 409, which contained sixth-graders. I had to wait at the desk without wiggling until Mr. Hilton, their teacher, had time to speak.

After five minutes he said, "Shirley?"

"What?" I whispered.

He said, "My! My! Shirley Abramowitz! They told me you had a particularly loud, clear voice and read with lots of expression. Could that be true?"

"Oh yes," I whispered.

"In that case, don't be silly; I might very well be your teacher someday. Speak up; speak up."

"Yes," I shouted.

"More like it," he said. "Now, Shirley, can you put a ribbon in your hair or a bobby pin? It's too messy."

"Yes!" I bawled.

"Now, now, calm down." He turned to the class. "Children, not a sound. Open at page 39. Read till 52. When you finish, start again." He looked me over once more. "Now, Shirley, you know, I suppose, that Christmas is coming. We are preparing a beautiful play. Most of the parts have been given out. But I still need a child with a strong voice, lots of stamina. Do you know what stamina is? You do? Smart kid. You know, I heard you read 'The Lord is my shepherd' in Assembly yesterday. I was very impressed. Wonderful delivery. Mrs. Jordan, your teacher, speaks highly of you. Now listen to me, Shirley Abramowitz, if you want to take the part and be in the play, repeat after me, 'I swear to work harder than I ever did before.'"

I looked to heaven and said at once, "Oh, I swear." I kissed my pinky and looked at God.

"That is an actor's life, my dear," he explained. "Like a soldier's, never tardy or disobedient to his general, the director. Everything," he said, "absolutely everything will depend on you."

That afternoon, all over the building, children scraped and scrubbed the turkeys and the sheaves of corn off the schoolroom windows. Goodbye Thanksgiving. The next morning a monitor brought red paper and green paper from the office. We made new shapes and hung them on the walls and glued them to the doors.

The teachers became happier and happier. Their heads were ringing like the bells of childhood. My best friend Evie was prone to evil, but she did not get a single demerit for whispering. We learned "Holy Night" without an error. "How wonderful!" said Miss Glacé, the student teacher. "To think that some of you don't even speak the language!" We learned "Deck the Halls" and "Hark! The Herald Angels" .... They weren't ashamed and we weren't embarrassed.

Oh, but when my mother heard about it all, she said to my father: "Misha, you don't know what's going on there. Cramer is the head of the Tickets Committee."

"Who?" asked my father. "Cramer? Oh yes, an active woman."

"Active? Active has to have a reason. Listen," she said sadly, "I'm surprised to see my neighbors making tra-la-la for Christmas."

My father couldn't think of what to say to that. Then he decided: "You're in America! Clara, you wanted to come here. In Palestine the Arabs would be eating you alive. Europe you had pogroms. Argentina is full of Indians. Here you got Christmas.... Some joke, ha?"

"Very funny, Misha. What is becoming of you? If we came to a new country a long time ago to run away from tyrants, and instead we fall into a creeping pogrom, that our children learn a lot of lies, so what's the joke? Ach, Misha, your idealism is going away."

"So is your sense of humor."

"That I never had, but idealism you had a lot of."

"I'm the same Misha Abramovitch, I didn't change an iota. Ask anyone."

"Only ask me," says my mama, may she rest in peace. "I got the answer."

Meanwhile the neighbors had to think of what to say too.

Marty's father said: "You know, he has a very important part, my boy."

"Mine also," said Mr. Sauerfeld.

"Not my boy!" said Mrs. Klieg. "I said to him no. The answer is no. When I say no! I mean no!"

The rabbi's wife said, "It's disgusting!" But no one listened to her. Under the narrow sky of God's great wisdom she wore a strawberry-blond wig.

Every day was noisy and full of experience. I was Right-hand Man. Mr. Hilton said: "How could I get along without you, Shirley?"

He said: "Your mother and father ought to get down on their knees every night and thank God for giving them a child like you."

He also said: "You're absolutely a pleasure to work with, my dear, dear child."

Sometimes he said: "For God's sakes, what did I do with the script? Shirley! Shirley! Find it."

Then I answered quietly: "Here it is, Mr. Hilton."

Once in a while, when he was very tired, he would cry out: "Shirley, I'm just tired of screaming at those kids. Will you tell Ira Pushkov not to come in till Lester points to that star the second time?"

Then I roared: "Ira Pushkov, what's the matter with you? Dope! Mr. Hilton told you five times already, don't come in till Lester points to that star the second time."

"Ach, Clara," my father asked, "what does she do there till six o'clock she can't even put the plates on the table?"

"Christmas," said my mother coldly.

"Ho! Ho!" my father said. "Christmas. What's the harm?

After all, history teaches everyone. We learn from reading this is a holiday from pagan times also, candles, lights, even Chanukah. So we learn it's not altogether Christian. So if they think it's a private holiday, they're only ignorant, not patriotic. What belongs to history, belongs to all men. You want to go back to the Middle Ages? Is it better to shave your head with a secondhand razor? Does it hurt Shirley to learn to speak up? It does not. So maybe someday she won't live between the kitchen and the shop. She's not a fool."

I thank you, Papa, for your kindness. It is true about me to this day. I am foolish but I am not a fool.

That night my father kissed me and said with great interest in my career, "Shirley, tomorrow's your big day. Congrats."

"Save it," my mother said. Then she shut all the windows in order to prevent tonsillitis.

In the morning it snowed. On the street corner a tree had been decorated for us by a kind city administration. In order to miss its chilly shadow our neighbors walked three blocks east to buy a loaf of bread. The butcher pulled down black window shades to keep the colored lights from shining on his chickens. Oh, not me. On the way to school, with both my hands I tossed it a kiss of tolerance. Poor thing, it was a stranger in Egypt.

I walked straight into the auditorium past the staring children. "Go ahead, Shirley!" said the monitors. Four boys, big for their age, had already started work as propmen and stagehands.

Mr. Hilton was very nervous. He was not even happy. Whatever he started to say ended in a sideward look of sadness. He sat slumped in the middle of the first row and asked me to help Miss Glacé. I did this, although she thought my voice too resonant and said, "Show-off!"

Parents began to arrive long before we were ready. They wanted to make a good impression. From among the yards of drapes I peeked out at the audience. I saw my embarrassed mother.

Ira, Lester, and Meyer were pasted to their beards by Miss Glacé. She almost forgot to thread the star on its wire, but I reminded her. I coughed a few times to clear my throat. Miss Glacé looked around and saw that everyone was in costume and on line waiting to play his part. She whispered, "All right . . ." Then:

Jackie Sauerfeld, the prettiest boy in first grade, parted the curtains with his skinny elbow and in a high voice sang out:

> *"Parents dear*
> *We are here*
> *To make a Christmas play in time.*
> *It we give*
> *In narrative*
> *And illustrate with pantomine."*

He disappeared.

My voice burst immediately from the wings to the great shock of Ira, Lester, and Meyer, who were waiting for it but were surprised all the same.

"I remember, I remember, the house where I was born . . ."

Miss Glacé yanked the curtain open and there it was,

the house—an old hayloft, where Celia Kornbluh lay in the straw with Cindy Lou, her favorite doll. Ira, Lester, and Meyer moved slowly from the wings toward her, sometimes pointing to a moving star and sometimes ahead to Cindy Lou.

It was a long story and it was a sad story. I carefully pronounced all the words about my lonesome childhood, while little Eddie Braunstein wandered upstage and down with his shepherd's stick, looking for sheep. I brought up lonesomeness again, and not being understood at all except by some women everybody hated. Eddie was too small for that and Marty Groff took his place, wearing his father's prayer shawl. I announced twelve friends, and half the boys in the fourth grade gathered round Marty, who stood on an orange crate while my voice harangued. Sorrowful and loud, I declaimed about love and God and Man, but because of the terrible deceit of Abie Stock we came suddenly to a famous moment. Marty, whose remembering tongue I was, waited at the foot of the cross. He stared desperately at the audience. I groaned, "My God, my God, why hast thou forsaken me?" The soldiers who were sheiks grabbed poor Marty to pin him up to die, but he wrenched free, turned again to the audience, and spread his arms aloft to show despair and the end. I murmured at the top of my voice, "The rest is silence, but as everyone in this room, in this city—in this world—now knows, I shall have life eternal."

That night Mrs. Kornbluh visited our kitchen for a glass of tea.

"How's the virgin?" asked my father with a look of concern.

"For a man with a daughter, you got a fresh mouth, Abramovitch."

"Here," said my father kindly, "have some lemon, it'll sweeten your disposition."

They debated a little in Yiddish, then fell in a puddle of Russian and Polish. What I understood next was my father, who said, "Still and all, it was certainly a beautiful affair, you have to admit, introducing us to the beliefs of a different culture."

"Well, yes," said Mrs. Kornbluh. "The only thing...you know Charlie Turner—that cute boy in Celia's class—a couple others? They got very small parts or no part at all. In very bad taste, it seemed to me. After all, it's their religion."

"Ach," explained my mother, "what could Mr. Hilton do? They got very small voices; after all, why should they holler? The English language they know from the beginning by heart. They're blond like angels. You think it's so important they should get in the play? Christmas...the whole piece of goods...they own it."

I listened and listened until I couldn't listen any more. Too sleepy, I climbed out of bed and kneeled. I made a little church of my hands and said, "Hear, O Israel..." Then I called out in Yiddish, "Please, good night, good night. Ssh." My father said, "Ssh yourself," and slammed the kitchen door.

I was happy. I fell asleep at once. I had prayed for everybody: my talking family, cousins far away, passersby, and all the lonesome Christians. I expected to be heard. My voice was certainly the loudest.

THANK YOU, M'AM

Langston Hughes

She was a large woman with a large purse that had everything in it but a hammer and nails. It had a long strap, and she carried it slung across her shoulder. It was about eleven o'clock at night, dark, and she was walking alone, when a boy ran up behind her and tried to snatch her purse. The strap broke with the sudden single tug the boy gave it from behind. But the boy's weight and the weight of the purse combined caused him to lose his balance. Instead of taking off full blast as he had hoped, the boy fell on his back on the sidewalk and his legs flew up. The large woman simply turned around and kicked him right square in his blue-jeaned sitter. Then she reached down, picked the boy up by his shirt front, and shook him until his teeth rattled.

After that the woman said, "Pick up my pocketbook, boy, and give it here."

She still held him tightly. But she bent down enough to permit him to stoop and pick up her purse. Then she said, "Now ain't you ashamed of yourself?"

Firmly gripped by his shirt front, the boy said, "Yes'm."

The woman said, "What did you want to do it for?"

The boy said, "I didn't aim to."

She said, "You a lie!"

By that time two or three people passed, stopped, turned to look, and some stood watching.

"If I turn you loose, will you run?" asked the woman.

"Yes'm," said the boy.

"Then I won't turn you loose," said the woman. She did not release him.

"Lady, I'm sorry," whispered the boy.

"Um-hum! Your face is dirty. I got a great mind to wash your face for you. Ain't you got nobody home to tell you to wash your face?"

"No'm," said the boy.

"Then it will get washed this evening," said the large woman, starting up the street, dragging the frightened boy behind her.

He looked as if he were fourteen or fifteen, frail and willow-wild, in tennis shoes and blue jeans.

The woman said, "You ought to be my son. I would teach you right from wrong. Least I can do right now is to wash your face. Are you hungry?"

"No'm," said the being-dragged boy. "I just want you to turn me loose."

"Was I bothering *you* when I turned that corner?" asked the woman.

"No'm."

"But you put yourself in contact with *me*," said the woman. "If you think that that contact is not going to last awhile, you got another thought coming. When I get through with you, sir, you are going to remember Mrs. Luella Bates Washington Jones."

Sweat popped out on the boy's face and he began to struggle. Mrs. Jones stopped, jerked him around in front of her, put a half nelson about his neck, and continued to drag him up the street. When she got to her door, she dragged the boy inside, down a hall, and into a large kitchenette-furnished room at the rear of the house. She switched on the light and left the door open. The boy could hear other roomers laughing and talking in the large house. Some of their doors were open, too, so he knew he and the woman were not alone. The woman still had him by the neck in the middle of her room.

She said, "What is your name?"

"Roger," answered the boy.

"Then, Roger, you go to that sink and wash your face," said the woman, whereupon she turned him loose—at last. Roger looked at the door—looked at the woman—looked at the door—*and went to the sink.*

"Let the water run until it gets warm," she said. "Here's a clean towel."

"You gonna take me to jail?" asked the boy, bending over the sink.

"Not with that face, I would not take you nowhere," said the woman. "Here I am trying to get home to cook me a bite to eat, and you snatch my pocketbook! Maybe you ain't been to your supper either, late as it be. Have you?"

"There's nobody home at my house," said the boy.

"Then we'll eat," said the woman. "I believe you're hungry—or been hungry—to try to snatch my pocketbook!"

"I want a pair of blue suede shoes," said the boy.

"Well, you didn't have to snatch *my* pocketbook to get some suede shoes," said Mrs. Luella Bates Washington Jones. "You could of asked me."

"M'am?"

The water dripping from his face, the boy looked at her. There was a long pause. A very long pause. After he had dried his face, and not knowing what else to do, dried it again, the boy turned around, wondering what next. The door was open. He could make a dash for it down the hall. He could run, run, run, *run!*

The woman was sitting on the daybed. After a while she said, "I were young once and I wanted things I could not get."

There was another long pause. The boy's mouth opened. Then he frowned, not knowing he frowned.

The woman said, "Um-hum! You thought I was going to say *but*, didn't you? You thought I was going to say, *but I didn't snatch people's pocketbooks*. Well, I wasn't going to say that." Pause. Silence. "I have done things, too, which I would not tell you, son—neither tell God, if He didn't already know. Everybody's got something in common. So you set down while I fix us something to eat. You might run that comb through your hair so you will look presentable."

In another corner of the room behind a screen was a gas plate and an icebox. Mrs. Jones got up and went behind the screen. The woman did not watch the boy to see if he was going to run now, nor did she watch her purse, which she left behind her on the daybed. But the boy took care to sit on the far side of the room, away from the purse, where he thought she could easily see him out of the corner of her eye if she wanted to. He did not trust the woman *not* to trust him. And he did not want to be mistrusted now.

"Do you need somebody to go to the store," asked the boy, "maybe to get some milk or something?"

"Don't believe I do," said the woman, "unless you just want sweet milk yourself. I was going to make cocoa out of this canned milk I got here."

"That will be fine," said the boy.

She heated some lima beans and ham she had in the icebox, made the cocoa, and set the table. The woman did not ask the boy anything about where he lived, or his folks, or anything else that would embarrass him. Instead, as they ate, she told him about her job in a hotel beauty shop that stayed open late, what the work was like, and how all kinds of women came in and out, blonds, redheads, and Spanish. Then she cut him a half of her ten-cent cake.

"Eat some more, son," she said.

When they were finished eating, she got up and said, "Now here, take this ten dollars and buy yourself some blue suede shoes. And next time, do not make the mistake of latching onto *my* pocketbook *nor nobody else's*—because shoes got by devilish ways will burn your feet. I got to get my rest now. But from here on in, son, I hope you will behave yourself."

She led him down the hall to the front door and opened it. "Good night! Behave yourself, boy!" she said, looking out into the street as he went down the steps.

The boy wanted to say something other than, "Thank you, M'am," to Mrs. Luella Bates Washington Jones, but although his lips moved, he couldn't even say that as he turned at the foot of the barren stoop and looked up at the large woman in the door. Then she shut the door.

THE ALL-AMERICAN SLURP

Lensey Namioka

The first time our family was invited out to dinner in America, we disgraced ourselves while eating celery. We had emigrated to this country from China, and during our early days here we had a hard time with American table manners.

In China we never ate celery raw, or any other kind of vegetable raw. We always had to disinfect the vegetables in boiling water first. When we were presented with our first relish tray, the raw celery caught us unprepared.

We had been invited to dinner by our neighbors, the Gleasons. After arriving at the house, we shook hands with our hosts and packed ourselves into a sofa. As our family of four sat stiffly in a row, my younger brother and I stole glances at our parents for a clue as to what to do next.

Mrs. Gleason offered the relish tray to Mother. The tray looked pretty, with its tiny red radishes, curly sticks of carrots, and long, slender stalks of pale green celery. "Do try some of the celery, Mrs. Lin," she said. "It's from a local farmer, and it's sweet."

Mother picked up one of the green stalks, and Father followed suit. Then I picked up a stalk, and my brother did too. So there we sat, each with a stalk of celery in our right hand.

Mrs. Gleason kept smiling. "Would you like to try some of the dip, Mrs. Lin? It's my own recipe: sour cream and onion flakes, with a dash of Tabasco sauce."

Most Chinese don't care for dairy products, and in those days I wasn't even ready to drink fresh milk. Sour cream sounded perfectly revolting. Our family shook our heads in unison.

Mrs. Gleason went off with the relish tray to the other guests, and we carefully watched to see what they did. Everyone seemed to eat the raw vegetables quite happily.

Mother took a bite of her celery. *Crunch.* "It's not bad!" she whispered.

Father took a bite of his celery. *Crunch.* "Yes, it *is* good," he said, looking surprised.

I took a bite, and then my brother. *Crunch, crunch.* It was more than good; it was delicious. Raw celery has a slight sparkle, a zingy taste that you don't get in cooked celery. When Mrs. Gleason came around with the relish tray, we each took another stalk of celery, except my brother. He took two.

There was only one problem: long strings ran through the length of the stalk, and they got caught in my teeth. When I help my mother in the kitchen, I always pull the strings out before slicing celery.

I pulled the strings out of my stalk. *Z-z-zip, z-z-zip.* My brother followed suit. *Z-z-zip, z-z-zip.* To my left, my parents were taking care of their own stalks. *Z-z-zip, z-z-zip, z-z-zip.*

Suddenly I realized that there was dead silence except for our zipping. Looking up, I saw that the eyes of everyone in the room were on our family. Mr. and Mrs. Gleason, their daughter Meg, who was my friend, and their neighbors the Badels—they were all staring at us as we busily pulled the strings of our celery.

That wasn't the end of it. Mrs. Gleason announced that dinner was served and invited us to the dining table. It was lavishly covered with platters of food, but we couldn't see any chairs around the table. So we helpfully carried over some dining chairs and sat down. All the other guests just stood there.

Mrs. Gleason bent down and whispered to us, "This is a buffet dinner. You help yourselves to some food and eat it in the living room."

Our family beat a retreat back to the sofa as if chased by enemy soldiers. For the rest of the evening, too mortified to go back to the dining table, I nursed a bit of potato salad on my plate.

Next day Meg and I got on the school bus together. I wasn't sure how she would feel about me after the spectacle our family made at the party. But she was just the same as usual, and the only reference she made to the party was, "Hope you and your folks got enough to eat last night. You certainly didn't take very much. Mom never tries to figure out how much food to prepare. She just puts everything on the table and hopes for the best."

I began to relax. The Gleasons' dinner party wasn't so different from a Chinese meal after all. My mother also puts everything on the table and hopes for the best.

Meg was the first friend I had made after we came to America. I eventually got acquainted with a few other kids in school, but Meg was still the only real friend I had.

My brother didn't have any problems making friends. He spent all his time with some boys who were teaching him baseball, and in no time he could speak English much faster than I could—not better, but faster.

I worried more about making mistakes, and I spoke carefully, making sure I could say everything right before opening my mouth. At least I had a better accent than my parents, who never really got rid of their Chinese accent, even years later. My parents had both studied English in school before coming to America, but what they had studied was mostly written English, not spoken.

Father's approach to English was a scientific one. Since Chinese verbs have no tense, he was fascinated by the way English verbs changed form according to whether they were in the present, past imperfect, perfect, pluperfect, future, or future perfect tense. He was always making diagrams of verbs and their inflections, and he looked for opportunities to show off his mastery of the pluperfect and future perfect tenses, his two favorites. "I shall have finished my project by Monday," he would say smugly.

Mother's approach was to memorize lists of polite phrases that would cover all possible social situations. She was constantly muttering things like "I'm fine, thank you. And you?" Once she accidentally stepped on someone's foot, and hurriedly blurted, "Oh, that's quite all right!" Embarrassed by her slip, she resolved to do better next time. So when someone stepped on *her* foot, she cried, "You're welcome!"

In our own different ways, we made progress in learning English. But I had another worry, and that was my appearance. My brother didn't have to worry, since Mother bought him blue jeans for school, and he dressed like all the other boys. But she insisted that girls had to wear skirts. By the time she saw that Meg and the other girls were wearing jeans, it was too late. My school clothes were bought already, and we didn't have money left to buy new outfits for me. We had too many other things to buy first, like furniture, pots, and pans.

The first time I visited Meg's house, she took me upstairs to her room, and I wound up trying on her clothes. We were pretty much the same size, since Meg was shorter and thinner than average. Maybe that's how we became friends in the first place. Wearing Meg's jeans and T-shirt, I looked at myself in the mirror. I could almost pass for an American—from the back, anyway. At least the kids in school wouldn't stop and stare at me in the hallways, which was what they did when they saw me in my white blouse and navy blue skirt that went a couple of inches below the knees.

When Meg came to my house, I invited her to try on my Chinese dresses, the ones with a high collar and slits up the sides. Meg's eyes were bright as she looked at herself in the mirror. She struck several sultry poses, and we nearly fell over laughing.

The dinner party at the Gleasons' didn't stop my growing friendship with Meg. Things were getting better for me in other ways too. Mother finally bought me some jeans at the end of the month, when Father got his paycheck. She wasn't in any hurry about buying them at first, until I worked on her. This is what I did. Since we didn't have a car in those days, I often ran down to the neighborhood store to pick up things for her. The groceries cost less at a big super-market, but the closest one was many blocks away. One day, when she ran out of flour, I offered to borrow a bike from our neighbor's son and buy a ten-pound bag of flour at the big supermarket. I mounted the boy's bike and waved to Mother. "I'll be back in five minutes!"

Before I started pedaling, I heard her voice behind me. "You can't go out in public like that! People can see all the way up to your thighs!"

"I'm sorry," I said innocently. "I thought you were in a hurry to get the flour." For dinner we were going to have pot-stickers (fried Chinese dumplings), and we needed a lot of flour.

"Couldn't you borrow a girl's bicycle?" complained Mother. "That way your skirt won't be pushed up."

"There aren't too many of those around," I said. "Almost

all the girls wear jeans while riding a bike, so they don't see any point buying a girl's bike."

We didn't eat pot-stickers that evening, and Mother was thoughtful. Next day we took the bus downtown and she bought me a pair of jeans. In the same week, my brother made the baseball team of his junior high school, Father started taking driving lessons, and Mother discovered rummage sales. We soon got all the furniture we needed, plus a dart board and a 1,000-piece jigsaw puzzle (fourteen hours later, we discovered that it was a 999-piece jigsaw puzzle). There was hope that the Lins might become a normal American family after all.

Then came our dinner at the Lakeview restaurant.

The Lakeview was an expensive restaurant, one of those places where a headwaiter dressed in tails conducted you to your seat, and the only light came from candles and flaming desserts. In one corner of the room a lady harpist played tinkling melodies.

Father wanted to celebrate, because he had just been promoted. He worked for an electronics company, and after his English started improving, his superiors decided to appoint him to a position more suited to his training. The promotion not only brought a higher salary but was also a tremendous boost to his pride.

Up to then we had eaten only in Chinese restaurants. Although my brother and I were becoming fond of hamburgers, my parents didn't care much for western food, other than chow mein.

But this was a special occasion, and Father asked his coworkers to recommend a really elegant restaurant. So there we were at the Lakeview, stumbling after the headwaiter in the murky dining room.

At our table we were handed our menus, and they were so big that to read mine I almost had to stand up again. But why bother? It was mostly in French, anyway.

Father, being an engineer, was always systematic. He took out a pocket French dictionary. "They told me that most of the items would be in French, so I came prepared." He even had a pocket flashlight, the size of a marking pen. While Mother held the flashlight over the menu, he looked up the items that were in French.

"*Pâté en croûte*," he muttered. "Let's see . . . *pâté* is paste . . . *croûte* is crust . . . hmm . . . a paste in crust."

The waiter stood looking patient. I squirmed and died at least fifty times.

At long last Father gave up. "Why don't we just order four complete dinners at random?" he suggested.

"Isn't that risky?" asked Mother. "The French eat some rather peculiar things, I've heard."

"A Chinese can eat anything a Frenchman can eat," Father declared.

The soup arrived in a plate. How do you get soup up from a plate? I glanced at the other diners, but the ones at the nearby tables were not on their soup course, while the more distant ones were invisible in the darkness.

Fortunately my parents had studied books on western etiquette before they came to America. "Tilt your plate," whispered my mother. "It's easier to spoon the soup up that way."

She was right. Tilting the plate did the trick. But the etiquette book didn't say anything about what you did after the soup reached your lips. As any respectable Chinese knows, the correct way to eat your soup is to slurp. This helps to cool the liquid and prevent you from burning your lips. It also shows your appreciation.

We showed our appreciation. *Shloop*, went my father. *Shloop*, went my mother. *Shloop*, *shloop*, went my brother, who was the hungriest.

The lady harpist stopped playing to take a rest. And in the silence, our family's consumption of soup suddenly seemed unnaturally loud. You know how it sounds on a rocky beach when the tide goes out and the water drains from all those little pools? They go *shloop*, *shloop*, *shloop*. That was the Lin family, eating soup.

At the next table a waiter was pouring wine. When a large *shloop* reached him, he froze. The bottle continued to pour, and red wine flooded the tabletop and into the lap of a customer. Even the customer didn't notice anything at first, being also hypnotized by the *shloop*, *shloop*, *shloop*.

It was too much. "I need to go to the toilet," I mumbled, jumping to my feet. A waiter, sensing my urgency, quickly directed me to the ladies' room.

I splashed cold water on my burning face, and as I dried myself with a paper towel, I stared into the mirror. In this perfumed ladies' room, with its pink-and-silver wallpaper and marbled sinks, I looked completely out of place. What was I doing here? What was our family doing in the Lakeview restaurant? In America?

The door to the ladies' room opened. A woman came

in and glanced curiously at me. I retreated into one of the toilet cubicles and latched the door.

Time passed—maybe half an hour, maybe an hour. Then I heard the door open again, and my mother's voice. "Are you in there? You're not sick, are you?"

There was real concern in her voice. A girl can't leave her family just because they slurp their soup. Besides, the toilet cubicle had a few drawbacks as a permanent residence. "I'm all right," I said, undoing the latch.

Mother didn't tell me how the rest of the dinner went, and I didn't want to know. In the weeks following, I managed to push the whole thing into the back of my mind, where it jumped out at me only a few times a day. Even now, I turn hot all over when I think of the Lakeview restaurant.

But by the time we had been in this country for three months, our family was definitely making progress toward becoming Americanized. I remember my parents' first PTA meeting. Father wore a neat suit and tie, and Mother put on her first pair of high heels. She stumbled only once. They met my homeroom teacher and beamed as she told them that I would make honor roll soon at the rate I was going. Of course Chinese etiquette forced Father to say that I was a very stupid girl and Mother to protest that the teacher was showing favoritism toward me. But I could tell they were both very proud.

The day came when my parents announced that they wanted to give a dinner party. We had invited Chinese friends to eat with us before, but this dinner was going to be different. In addition to a Chinese-American family, we were going to invite the Gleasons.

"Gee, I can hardly wait to have dinner at your house," Meg said to me. "I just *love* Chinese food."

That was a relief. Mother was a good cook, but I wasn't sure if people who ate sour cream would also eat chicken gizzards stewed in soy sauce.

Mother decided not to take a chance with chicken gizzards. Since we had western guests, she set the table with large dinner plates, which we never used in Chinese meals. In fact we didn't use individual plates at all, but picked up food from the platters in the middle of the table and brought it directly to our rice bowls. Following the practice of Chinese-American restaurants, Mother also placed large serving spoons on the platters.

The dinner started well. Mrs. Gleason exclaimed at the beautifully arranged dishes of food: the colorful candied fruit in the sweet-and-sour pork dish, the noodle-thin shreds of chicken meat stir-fried with tiny peas, and the glistening pink prawns in a ginger sauce.

At first I was too busy enjoying my food to notice how the guests were doing. But soon I remembered my duties. Sometimes guests were too polite to help themselves and you had to serve them with more food.

I glanced at Meg, to see if she needed more food, and my eyes nearly popped out at the sight of her plate. It was piled with food: the sweet-and-sour meat pushed right against the chicken shreds, and the chicken sauce ran into the prawns. She had been taking food from a second dish before she finished eating her helping from the first!

Horrified, I turned to look at Mrs. Gleason. She was dumping rice out of her bowl and putting it on her dinner plate. Then she ladled prawns and gravy on top of the rice and mixed everything together, the way you mix sand, gravel, and cement to make concrete.

I couldn't bear to look any longer, and I turned to Mr. Gleason. He was chasing a pea around his plate. Several times he got it to the edge, but when he tried to pick it up with his chopsticks, it rolled back toward the center of the plate again. Finally he put down his chopsticks and picked up the pea with his fingers. He really did! A grown man!

All of us, our family and the Chinese guests, stopped eating to watch the activities of the Gleasons. I wanted to giggle. Then I caught my mother's eyes on me. She frowned and shook her head slightly, and I understood the message: the Gleasons were not used to Chinese ways, and they were just coping the best they could. For some reason I thought of celery strings.

When the main courses were finished, Mother brought out a platter of fruit. "I hope you weren't expecting a sweet dessert," she said. "Since the Chinese don't eat dessert, I didn't think to prepare any."

"Oh, I couldn't possibly eat dessert!" cried Mrs. Gleason. "I'm simply stuffed!"

Meg had different ideas. When the table was cleared, she announced that she and I were going for a walk. "I don't know about you, but I feel like dessert," she told me, when we were outside. "Come on, there's a Dairy Queen down the street. I could use a big chocolate milkshake!"

Although I didn't really want anything more to eat,

I insisted on paying for the milkshakes. After all, I was still hostess.

Meg got her large chocolate milkshake and I had a small one. Even so, she was finishing hers while I was only half done. Toward the end she pulled hard on her straws and went *shloop, shloop.*

"Do you always slurp when you eat a milkshake?" I asked, before I could stop myself.

Meg grinned. "Sure. All Americans slurp."

THE NO-GUITAR BLUES

Gary Soto

The moment Fausto saw the group Los Lobos on "American Bandstand," he knew exactly what he wanted to do with his life—play guitar. His eyes grew large with excitement as Los Lobos ground out a song while teenagers bounced off each other on the crowded dance floor.

He had watched "American Bandstand" for years and had heard Ray Camacho and the Teardrops at Romain Playground, but it had never occurred to him that he too might become a musician. That afternoon Fausto knew his mission in life: to play guitar in his own band; to sweat out his songs and prance around the stage; to make money and dress weird.

Fausto turned off the television set and walked outside, wondering how he could get enough money to buy a guitar. He couldn't ask his parents because they would just say, "Money doesn't grow on trees" or "What do you think we are, bankers?" And besides, they hated rock music. They were into the *conjunto* music of Lydia Mendoza, Flaco Jimenez, and Little Joe and La Familia. And, as Fausto recalled, the last album they bought was *The Chipmunks Sing Christmas Favorites*.

But what the heck, he'd give it a try. He returned inside and watched his mother make tortillas. He leaned against the kitchen counter, trying to work up the nerve to ask her for a guitar. Finally, he couldn't hold back any longer.

"Mom," he said, "I want a guitar for Christmas."

She looked up from rolling tortillas. "Honey, a guitar costs a lot of money."

"How 'bout for my birthday next year," he tried again.

"I can't promise," she said, turning back to her tortillas, "but we'll see."

Fausto walked back outside with a buttered tortilla. He knew his mother was right. His father was a warehouseman at Berven Rugs, where he made good money but not enough to buy everything his children wanted. Fausto decided to mow lawns to earn money, and was pushing the mower down the street before he realized it was winter and no one would hire him. He returned the mower and picked up a rake. He hopped onto his sister's bike (his had two flat tires) and rode north to the nicer section of Fresno in search of work. He went door-to-door, but after three hours he managed to get only one job, and not to rake leaves. He was asked to hurry down to the store to buy a loaf of bread, for which he received a grimy, dirt-caked quarter.

He also got an orange, which he ate sitting at the curb. While he was eating, a dog walked up and sniffed his leg. Fausto pushed him away and threw an orange peel skyward. The dog caught it and ate it in one gulp. The dog looked at Fausto and wagged his tail for more. Fausto tossed him a slice of orange, and the dog snapped it up and licked his lips.

"How come you like oranges, dog?"

The dog blinked a pair of sad eyes and whined.

"What's the matter? Cat got your tongue?" Fausto laughed at his joke and offered the dog another slice.

At that moment a dim light came on inside Fausto's head. He saw that it was sort of a fancy dog, a terrier or something, with dog tags and a shiny collar. And it looked well fed and healthy. In his neighborhood, the dogs were never licensed, and if they got sick they were placed near the water heater until they got well.

This dog looked like he belonged to rich people. Fausto cleaned his juice-sticky hands on his pants and got to his feet. The light in his head grew brighter. It just might work. He called the dog, patted its muscular back, and bent down to check the license.

"Great," he said. "There's an address."

The dog's name was Roger, which struck Fausto as weird because he'd never heard of a dog with a human name. Dogs should have names like Bomber, Freckles, Queenie, Killer, and Zero.

Fausto planned to take the dog home and collect a reward. He would say he had found Roger near the freeway. That would scare the daylights out of the owners, who would be so happy that they would probably give him a reward. He felt bad about lying, but the dog *was* loose. And it might even really be lost, because the address was six blocks away.

Fausto stashed the rake and his sister's bike behind a bush, and, tossing an orange peel every time Roger became distracted, walked the dog to his house. He hesitated on the porch until Roger began to scratch the door with a muddy paw. Fausto had come this far, so he figured he might as well go through with it. He knocked softly. When no one answered, he rang the doorbell. A man in a silky bathrobe and slippers opened the door and seemed confused by the sight of his dog and the boy.

"Sir," Fausto said, gripping Roger by the collar. "I found your dog by the freeway. His dog license says he lives here." Fausto looked down at the dog, then up to the man. "He does, doesn't he?"

The man stared at Fausto a long time before saying in a pleasant voice, "That's right." He pulled his robe tighter around him because of the cold and asked Fausto to come in. "So he was by the freeway?"

"Uh-huh."

"You bad, snoopy dog," said the man, wagging his finger. "You probably knocked over some trash cans, too, didn't you?"

Fausto didn't say anything. He looked around, amazed by this house with its shiny furniture and a television as large as the front window at home. Warm bread smells filled the air and music full of soft tinkling floated in from another room.

"Helen," the man called to the kitchen. "We have a visitor." His wife came into the living room wiping her hands on a dish towel and smiling. "And who have we here?" she asked in one of the softest voices Fausto had ever heard.

"This young man said he found Roger near the freeway."

Fausto repeated his story to her while staring at a perpetual clock with a bell-shaped glass, the kind his aunt got when she celebrated her twenty-fifth anniversary. The lady frowned and said, wagging a finger at Roger, "Oh, you're a bad boy."

"It was very nice of you to bring Roger home," the man said. "Where do you live?"

"By that vacant lot on Olive," he said. "You know, by Brownie's Flower Place."

The wife looked at her husband, then Fausto. Her eyes twinkled triangles of light as she said, "Well, young man, you're probably hungry. How about a turnover?"

"What do I have to turn over?" Fausto asked, thinking she was talking about yard work or something like turning over trays of dried raisins.

"No, no, dear, it's a pastry." She took him by the elbow and guided him to a kitchen that sparkled with copper pans and bright yellow wallpaper. She guided him to the kitchen table and gave him a tall glass of milk and something that looked like an *empanada*. Steamy waves of heat escaped when he tore it in two. He ate with both eyes on the man and woman who stood arm in arm smiling at him. They were strange, he thought. But nice.

"That was good," he said after he finished the turnover. "Did you make it, ma'am?"

"Yes, I did. Would you like another?"

"No, thank you. I have to go home now."

As Fausto walked to the door, the man opened his wallet and took out a bill. "This is for you," he said. "Roger is very special to us, almost like a son."

Fausto looked at the bill and knew he was in trouble. Not with these nice folks or with his parents but with himself. How could he have been so deceitful? The dog wasn't lost. It was just having a fun Saturday walking around.

"I can't take that."

"You have to. You deserve it, believe me," the man said.

"No, I don't."

"Now don't be silly," said the lady. She took the bill from her husband and stuffed it into Fausto's shirt pocket. "You're a lovely child. Your parents are lucky to have you. Be good. And come see us again, please."

Fausto went out, and the lady closed the door. Fausto clutched the bill through his shirt pocket. He felt like ringing the doorbell and begging them to please take the money back, but he knew they would refuse. He hurried away, and at the end of the block, pulled the bill from his shirt pocket: it was a crisp twenty-dollar bill.

"Oh, man, I shouldn't have lied," he said under his breath as he started up the street like a zombie. He wanted to run to church for Saturday confession, but it was past four-thirty, when confession stopped.

He returned to the bush where he had hidden the rake and his sister's bike and rode home slowly, not daring to touch the money in his pocket. At home, in the privacy of his room, he examined the twenty-dollar bill. He had never had so much money. It was probably enough to buy a secondhand guitar. But he felt bad, like the time he stole a dollar from the secret fold inside his older brother's wallet.

Fausto went outside and sat on the fence. "Yeah," he said. "I can probably get a guitar for twenty. Maybe at a yard sale—things are cheaper."

His mother called him to dinner.

The next day he dressed for church without anyone telling him. He was going to go to eight o'clock mass.

"I'm going to church, Mom," he said. His mother was in the kitchen cooking *papas* and *chorizo con huevos*. A pile of tortillas lay warm under a dishtowel.

"Oh, I'm so proud of you, my son." She beamed, turning over the crackling *papas*.

His older brother, Lawrence, who was at the table reading the funnies, mimicked, "Oh, I'm so proud of you, my son," under his breath.

At Saint Theresa's he sat near the front. When Father Jerry began by saying that we are all sinners, Fausto thought he looked straight at him. Could he know? Fausto fidgeted with guilt. No, he thought. I only did it yesterday.

Fausto knelt, prayed, and sang. But he couldn't forget the man and the lady, whose names he didn't even know, and the *empanada* they had given him. It had a strange name but tasted really good. He wondered how they got rich. And how that dome clock worked. He had asked his mother once how his aunt's clock worked. She said it just worked, the way the refrigerator works. It just did.

Fausto caught his mind wandering and tried to concentrate on his sins. He said a Hail Mary and sang, and when the wicker basket came his way, he stuck a hand reluctantly in his pocket and pulled out the twenty-dollar bill. He ironed it between his palms, and dropped it into the basket. The grownups stared. Here was a kid dropping twenty dollars in the basket while they gave just three or four dollars.

There would be a second collection for Saint Vincent de Paul, the lector announced. The wicker baskets again floated in the pews, and this time the adults around him, given a second chance to show their charity, dug deep into their wallets and purses and dropped in fives and tens. This time Fausto tossed in the grimy quarter.

Fausto felt better after church. He went home and played football in the front yard with his brother and some neighbor kids. He felt cleared of wrongdoing and was so happy that he played one of his best games of football ever. On one play, he tore his good pants, which he knew he shouldn't have been wearing. For a second, while he examined the hole, he wished he hadn't given the twenty dollars away.

Man, I coulda bought me some Levi's, he thought. He pictured his twenty dollars being spent to buy church candles. He pictured a priest buying an armful of flowers with *his* money.

Fausto had to forget about getting a guitar. He spent the next day playing soccer in his good pants, which were now his old pants. But that night during dinner, his mother said she remembered seeing an old bass guitarron the last time she cleaned out her father's garage.

"It's a little dusty," his mom said, serving his favorite enchiladas, "But I think it works. Grandpa says it works."

Fausto's ears perked up. That was the same kind the guy in Los Lobos played. Instead of asking for the guitar, he waited for his mother to offer it to him. And she did, while gathering the dishes from the table.

"No, Mom, I'll do it," he said, hugging her. "I'll do the dishes forever if you want."

It was the happiest day of his life. No, it was the second-happiest day of his life. The happiest was when his grandfather Lupe placed the guitarron, which was nearly as huge as a washtub, in his arms. Fausto ran a thumb down the strings, which vibrated in his throat and chest. It sounded beautiful, deep and eerie. A pumpkin smile widened on his face.

"Okay, *hijo*, now you put your fingers like this," said his grandfather, smelling of tobacco and aftershave. He took Fausto's fingers and placed them on the strings. Fausto strummed a chord on the guitarron, and the bass resounded in their chests.

The guitarron was more complicated than Fausto imagined. But he was confident that after a few more lessons he could start a band that would someday play on "American Bandstand" for the dancing crowds.

SIXTH GRADE

Michele Wallace

I can remember the details but I never do when I think of the episode at all. I remember the feeling and it must have been painful because it hurts now to try to remember the details of exactly what happened.

I had a group of friends that I talked with. All my friends were girls in the sixth grade because the boys would hit you and get your dress dirty. I had never had a group of friends before and I wanted to forget a few things. I had wet my pants at least once every year I had been in that school; whenever a teacher wanted to hit me with a paddle they had to chase me around the room and they rarely caught me and if they did I yelled so loud they had to leave me alone. The kids were still laughing about the latter incidents but I hadn't wet my pants yet this year and it was already October. No one brought that up any more.

My friends and I had a club that was my idea. You had to chew thirteen pieces of bubble gum every day to join. I loved bubble gum. We weren't supposed to chew gum in class. Of course, I got caught and I had to stay after school for an hour and I cried but the teacher didn't care. So I swallowed a piece of a plastic pen and then I told her. She let me go home, said I should see a doctor. I never did. The piece was small.

I don't know why my friends liked me, but they were always laughing when I was around so I guess I was funny. They thought I was kind, I think. I screamed at our enemies, cried whenever anybody tried to hurt any one of us. I was different and they liked that, sometimes; I could always tell them about things they didn't know already.

I was eleven and I was becoming shy. Before, it never bothered me that every move I made was news for the entire staff and student body of that little lily-white Lutheran school way up in the then safe and silent Bronx. When I reached the sixth grade, it all became very important. I was madly jealous of their little red brick homes in neat little rows near the school with little Dicks, Janes, and Spots running around everywhere, of their housewife mothers who met them after school, of their crisp, immaculate box lunches with clean wax paper packages of Lifesavers, of their Thom McAn shoes, of their clean white blouses with peter pan collars, and their fresh cotton dresses in summer and winter alike, and their white ankle socks, of their small, clear, light print on totally unblemished standard lined notebook paper in their plastic covered super large and cute looseleafs, of their perfect homework in Bic blue ink and their little brothers and sisters who were convenient and silent versions of themselves.

Whereas I lived in a tall apartment building with a monumental elevator, all of which was an uncomfortably long and lonely bus distance away from the school. I had the El train, other apartment buildings, pigeons who frightened you and did their thing on your head, push-open windows, and kids I didn't know for company. My mother was an art teacher at a public school nowhere near my school, and she used the dinette for a studio, and she and all the walls were always covered with paint. I usually forgot to bring my lunch but when I did, it had been bought at a Puerto Rican delicatessen across the street from my house and it was always a liverwurst hero with lots of mayonnaise and very little lettuce—no white bread, no unwrinkled cellophane wrappers around Lifesavers, or cucumbers or cupcakes, or anything else; or when my mother made my lunch, which was rare, really rare, it was a ham and cheese sandwich with the bread missing, or the ham missing, or the cheese missing and no dessert. I was allergic to the milk that everybody drank which came in little red and white wax containers. Even the teacher drank it, but once in the second grade I had shaved the wax from the container and placed it in a neat pile in the center of my desk where the teacher could see it plainly. I looked up at her frequently waiting for her signal of approval and admiration of such genius. She hit me with a paddle with a smiling face painted on it. She pulled my dress up and put me over her knee in front of the whole class. She caught me because I didn't run—it was my first year in the school. My lunch was always in a brown paper bag. My shoes were sturdy and lasted forever, no laces, just buckles. Most of my clothes were made by my grandmother—wool dresses in the winter, cotton dresses in the summer, and they were all my grandmother's own styles, styles that no one, no one had ever seen in the Fordham Road part of the Bronx. Nothing I ever wore was white, at least not for long. I wore colors, lots of pink, orange and red, and all together, and lots of crinoline slips and short, short, everything short. I wore tights, no socks. I had them in every color in the rainbow. My teacher hated tights. I know because she told me so, me and the rest of the class. I wrote with my left hand and my handwriting was heavy and crossed out a lot. My teacher told us never to cross out, always erase. My erasers were dirty. My paper either had no lines, or no holes for the looseleaf, or not enough holes but never too many (of course you can never have too many). I never got a looseleaf till at least a month after school started, and even then it wasn't big enough, it definitely didn't have any pretty designs, and I usually lost it. My homework was always done in red or brown ink or with an etching pen, and longterm assignments included my drawings and my own interpretation of the project, and they were late anyway. My little sister wasn't little enough; she was only eleven months younger than I was. She cried constantly, ran up and down the halls, said rude things at the wrong time, wore polka dotted blouses half in and half out of her plaid skirts, her socks down in her shoes. You always had to repeat things for her twice because the first time she was dreaming. She said things that were not true and talked about me all the time. She pointed me out to everybody she knew, and didn't know, ran after me yelling that she loved me, kissed me goodbye in the morning, came to my classroom and asked for me whenever she could get away, and stood around after school telling me that Mommy said that we should always come home together and right away.

So you see, I was different. Other kids were different too, I know, but everybody in the school didn't know about it. Like this one little Irish girl—her mother was a prostitute and an alcoholic, but what kid knew it in the school? She said her father was the Bailey of Barnum and Bailey and that she was in the circus. Nobody ever saw her father and everybody sat too high up in Madison Square Garden to swear she wasn't in the show. She showed us all pictures of herself with sailors who were her friends when she was little. Everybody did know she was a little different. But my sister and I were first-class entertainment.

I tried to change. I asked my mother to buy a house. Whenever anybody brought my sister up in conversation, I changed the topic to how I had gone to Europe that summer, and how good the ice cream was there. They listened and they forgot a little.

But that wasn't enough for the staff of the school, especially my teacher; they couldn't hear me. You see, they looked down at me, and when they did, it was to say something to me, not to hear me say something, except perhaps a phrase from the catechism, or one of the hymns. They were

not at all happy with me. Although I had a good memory
for Bible passages, my attendance was poor in school and
in church. My mother was not a churchgoer, and didn't
have the heart to force us to go. If it rained or snowed
heavily, or Barbara and I wanted to be with her, we didn't
always have to go to school. In the morning, we would stay
home and talk with her and read, and she would put on
musical plays for us while we pretended we were sick. In
the afternoon we would go shopping downtown, or to a
museum, or the zoo, or to buy art supplies, or to F.A.O.
Schwarz to look at toy trains. When we came to school, we
were late but they couldn't kick us out because we could
read and write and spell and do arithmetic better than most
of the kids who came every day. If they put us in the fast
part of the class, we got bored and didn't do our homework
and failed our tests, but if they put us in the slow part of
the class, we intimidated the kids there. Our marks went
from A to F to A, from day to day. Our teachers were in a
frenzy. They couldn't say we were non-believers because
both of us were religious fanatics, and would render a prayer
at the appearance of the merest need. When we didn't go
to church, Barbara and I held our own private services on
Sunday mornings while our mother slept. Mother told us
to lie about church but we never did. Our teachers were
dismayed. They couldn't say we were evil or malicious or
that we frightened other children or beat them up. We were
always disobeying orders, but then we were always sorry,
and we would cry until we had proved it. We would give
all our money and pencils and lunch (if we had any) and
paper (clean or dirty) to anybody. We never hit anyone, we

got hit; and when we did, we ran to the teacher. Our teachers were helpless. They couldn't say we were backward or retarded because we were extremely vocal and prolific on all kinds of subjects like the Uffizi Galleries in Florence, the New York subways and Forty-second Street. We did fantastically well on all non-credit tests. We never hesitated to defend our rights, at least not until I was in the sixth grade. Out teachers gave up all hope then.

My teacher that sixth year was different from the rest of the teachers there. She was disgusted and repelled by my sister and me, and she showed it sometimes, too. She was young, about twenty-seven. I think she told us her age but maybe she didn't. I was good at age guessing, even then. To me, she was striking and handsome, the career girl in the movies. Her eyes were blue; they were cold and at the same time piercing. When she was angry, she would pull her nondescript chin as far as possible into her slender, long, by then, strawberry neck. Her nostrils would puff with air and stain red, and it was as if her eyes would reach out with a surgical instrument to pick away at whatever it was in you that was annoying her. She had patience; she had concentration. She would not give up the manipulation of her powerful instrument until either the individual had removed himself or herself from her sight, or had repressed that element of his or her character to her satisfaction. One had to give up to her magnetic grasp. To me in the sixth grade, a little black girl who was used to smiles and hugs and kisses, all of this registered not as an image but as a situation, situation red—danger. I was afraid, scared of her, and I hadn't mastered yet the kind of repression that she demanded; but I was learning. Perhaps if she had gone a little slower with me. I needed time: she didn't have it. She didn't like me. She intrigued me. I know no other word.

She was slim and tall and she stood up straight. Her ancestors were Irish and German. Her name was Miss Kenny the first year she taught at Our Savior Lutheran School. The next year she got married and she had me in her class. Her name was Mrs. Wernerhann. Her husband was German. The kids who hated her called her Mrs. Watermelon. Her husband came to school for a watermelon party we had at the end of the year; nobody said anything. I don't remember her voice but its quality was crisp, clear cut with a definite period at the end of each sentence. She talked a lot, not about history or religion, but about the college she went to and particularly her sorority. I was fascinated by her description of the initiation. We all admired her endurance and bravery, and were anxious to prove ours as soon as possible in a similar initiation process.

I can only remember two things she ever said directly to me. One was about a science notebook that we had to do some assignment in every day, and at the end of the week we had to pass it in to her so she could check it. I went to her desk to give her mine. She took it and smiled the only way she knew how and said, indicating pleased amazement: "Your notebook is always so neat, Sandra." Then she looked down at it. There was a gravy stain on the cover. I was smart; I turned my back on her instrument; it felt me but I ignored it. I was silent, smileless. Before, I always smiled. Before, I always had something to say. Now

I was silent and smileless. I guess she was satisfied for the moment. She turned her attentions to another student.

The other time that I remember, she was indulging in a vulgar habit that all the teachers seemed to have in that school. She was reading aloud the names of each student along with the grade that kid had received on his last quiz. There was frequent quizzing in her class. She read my grade. It was 100 and my grades for quite a time had been 100, but it was still quite early in the year. Nevertheless, I did want to impress her. She was impressed. I remember her words exactly. This time I was seated near the back of the room, minding my own business, trying to read my book and forget that she was reading the grades. Other kids were doing likewise or otherwise, but whatever they were doing, all were doing it quietly, very quietly. Mrs. Wernerhann did not permit any noise in her classroom. "Why Sandra, I'm amazed. I thought certainly you would be one of my F students." The class laughed carelessly, as if they hadn't laughed in years and years and were desperate to find something funny, anything; they would laugh at anything, and this was just as funny as anything. Actually I don't remember how they laughed; it wasn't thunder in my ears but I know they laughed, I know.

Did she look up my record? She didn't look up my record, because if she did, she would have seen that I'm real smart underneath. She didn't know me before. She only paid attention to her class, only. Did she hear about me? What did she hear? Maybe she heard, but mostly she saw, the lady could see real good.

•

She was looking at me. Her voice was at attention. She smiled. I smiled. She read the next name, the next grade. She had caught me silent, smileless. I talked only to my friends. I even listened to them more. I never talked to her. I blended more, or I thought I was blending. I tried.

It was near Halloween and my class was going to have a party. During our recess period we went to the park near the school. She broke the class up into committees for planning the party. One committee, with all my friends on it, was hanging on the fence. It was one of those wire-woven fences with big empty spaces that we could put our small hands through and climb and pull on. It was invitation; everybody hung on the fence. She was discussing something with one of the committees. I hadn't been placed on a committee; I knew that I should be afraid. I approached her from behind. I tapped her lightly. "Mrs. Wernerhann, Mrs. Wernerhann." I said it softly. No response. I came round to the front. "Mrs. Wernerhann, you haven't assigned me to any committee." I said this softly, too. No response. I repeated my words even more softly, slowly, searching for my error in tone, grammar, pronunciation, attitude. She glanced at me for just a moment, the instrument waving at me: it didn't have time. She continued to address her attentive group who followed suit and ignored me. Actually, I don't know what they did, but they sure didn't stop and ask me what it was that I wanted. I searched frantically— my appearance, my hair, my clothes, my smell, me, me, me, me. This time she had not silenced me. I had come to her silent. It was a kind of victory, I guess, but it was empty. I came without an answer. I was asking. Now my thoughts reached to the end, to the end of that recess period, to the end of the school, to the end of her, to darkness and noise too, and for now, to the fence, and thereafter would blend into chairs, walls, whatever would answer my silence with silence.

I went home. My mother always asked me every day what had happened to me in school, and then she would tell me what had happened to her in school that day. We always talked like this. I told her what had happened. She talked to me and I listened to her. I talked to her. We logically figured it out; Mrs. Wernerhann was wrong to have hurt me. Who said pain? She held me. I don't remember her touching me. She felt I had a fever. She told me to go to bed. I did.

I cried there, softly so my mother couldn't hear me, although she probably did. I had never cried in bed before, except with a book. It didn't feel like a step forward. I slipped into a martyred bliss. I am sure I was not sleeping. I must have been thinking about religion. My bed was my place to think about the "whys" for everything. Why do people look the way they do? Why are there people? Why are there children and adults? Why is my skin black? Now I was just thinking. "Why?" That was new, too. It didn't feel good. Why? I was asking why? I closed my eyes. It felt good and all right. There were arms around me, my own. I opened my eyes, my hands were stretched out in front of me. They were not my arms. They couldn't be anyway; these arms were too large and soft and warm, and I was skinny and puny. But that was not the question. I had been answered.

My mother went to school the next day. She spoke to
Mrs. Wernerhann about children. She did not ask for love;
I didn't understand that. Instead she asked for dignity and
respect, placing the doubt on Mrs. Wernerhann's profes-
sional integrity, rather than on her supply of compassion.
Just as my mother reached the door, Mrs. Wernerhann
exploded: "Why don't you go to the NAACP?" She had to.
My mother was not interested in her silent instrument. My
mother, she turned around, she did not speak, she laughed
in her face, curiously and in operatic tones (as was her
manner when she was disturbed) and then left to go see
the principal. He spoke mostly of God and love. My mother
arranged a meeting with the pastor of our church, the principal, Mrs. Wernerhann, and herself. The two men made
silent agreements on the topic for discussion; it was to be
God and love. Mrs. Wernerhann was silent. Nobody wanted
to talk about me. They asked my mother for her patience,
her love and faith. It would take time. My mother did not
have it.

As far as I know, I left that school that day in the park,
but I stayed to the end of the year. I never went back to
church. I soon moved away from the Bronx.

PRESIDENT CLEVELAND, WHERE ARE YOU?

Robert Cormier

That was the autumn of the cowboy cards—Buck Jones and Tom Tyler and Hoot Gibson and especially Ken Maynard. The cards were available in those five-cent packages of gum: pink sticks, three together, covered with a sweet white powder. You couldn't blow bubbles with that particular gum, but it couldn't have mattered less. The cowboy cards were important—the pictures of those rock-faced men with eyes of blue steel.

On those windswept, leaf-tumbling afternoons we gathered after school on the sidewalk in front of Lemire's Drugstore, across from St. Jude's Parochial School, and we swapped and bargained and matched for the cards. Because

a Ken Maynard serial was playing at the Globe every Saturday afternoon, he was the most popular cowboy of all, and
one of his cards was worth at least ten of any other kind.
Rollie Tremaine had a treasure of thirty or so, and he
guarded them jealously. He'd match you for the other cards,
but he risked his Ken Maynards only when the other kids
threatened to leave him out of the competition altogether.

You could almost hate Rollie Tremaine. In the first
place, he was the only son of Auguste Tremaine, who oper-
ated the Uptown Dry Goods Store, and he did not live in a
tenement but in a big white birthday cake of a house on
Laurel Street. He was too fat to be effective in the football
games between the Frenchtown Tigers and the North Side
Knights, and he made us constantly aware of the jingle of
coins in his pockets. He was able to stroll into Lemire's and
casually select a quarter's worth of cowboy cards while the
rest of us watched, aching with envy.

Once in a while I earned a nickel or dime by running
errands or washing windows for blind old Mrs. Belander,
or by finding pieces of copper, brass, and other valuable
metals at the dump and selling them to the junkman. The
coins clutched in my hand, I would race to Lemire's to buy
a cowboy card or two, hoping that Ken Maynard would
stare boldly out at me as I opened the pack. At one time,
before a disastrous matching session with Roger Lussier
(my best friend, except where the cards were involved), I
owned five Ken Maynards and considered myself a million-
aire, of sorts.

One week I was particularly lucky; I had spent two
afternoons washing floors for Mrs. Belander and received a

quarter. Because my father had worked a full week at the shop, where a rush order for fancy combs had been received, he allotted my brothers and sisters and me an extra dime along with the usual ten cents for the Saturday-afternoon movie. Setting aside the movie fare, I found myself with a bonus of thirty-five cents, and I then planned to put Rollie Tremaine to shame the following Monday afternoon.

Monday was the best day to buy the cards because the candy man stopped at Lemire's every Monday morning to deliver the new assortments. There was nothing more exciting in the world than a fresh batch of card boxes. I rushed home from school that day and hurriedly changed my clothes, eager to set off for the store. As I burst through the doorway, letting the screen door slam behind me, my brother Armand blocked my way.

He was fourteen, three years older than I, and a freshman at Monument High School. He had recently become a stranger to me in many ways—indifferent to such matters as cowboy cards and the Frenchtown Tigers—and he carried himself with a mysterious dignity that was fractured now and then when his voice began shooting off in all directions like some kind of vocal fireworks.

"Wait a minute, Jerry," he said. "I want to talk to you." He motioned me out of earshot of my mother, who was busy supervising the usual after-school skirmish in the kitchen.

I sighed with impatience. In recent months Armand had become a figure of authority, siding with my father and mother occasionally. As the oldest son he sometimes took advantage of his age and experience to issue rules and regulations.

"How much money have you got?" he whispered.

"You in some kind of trouble?" I asked, excitement rising in me as I remembered the blackmail plot of a movie at the Globe a month before.

He shook his head in annoyance. "Look," he said, "it's Pa's birthday tomorrow. I think we ought to chip in and buy him something..."

I reached into my pocket and caressed the coins. "Here," I said carefully, pulling out a nickel. "If we all give a nickel we should have enough to buy him something pretty nice."

He regarded me with contempt. "Rita already gave me fifteen cents, and I'm throwing in a quarter. Albert handed over a dime—all that's left of his birthday money. Is that all you can do—a nickel?"

"Aw, come on," I protested. "I haven't got a single Ken Maynard left, and I was going to buy some cards this afternoon."

"Ken Maynard!" he snorted. "Who's more important—him or your father?"

His question was unfair because he knew that there was no possible choice—"my father" had to be the only answer. My father was a huge man who believed in the things of the spirit, although my mother often maintained that the spirits he believed in came in bottles. He had worked at the Monument Comb Shop since the age of fourteen; his booming laugh—or grumble—greeted us each night when he returned from the factory. A steady worker when the shop had enough work, he quickened with gaiety on Friday nights and weekends, a bottle of beer at his elbow, and he was fond of making long speeches about the good things in life. In the middle of the Depression, for instance, he paid cash for a piano, of all things, and insisted that my twin sisters, Yolande and Yvette, take lessons once a week.

I took a dime from my pocket and handed it to Armand.

"Thanks, Jerry," he said. "I hate to take your last cent."

"That's all right," I replied, turning away and consoling myself with the thought that twenty cents was better than nothing at all.

When I arrived at Lemire's I sensed disaster in the air. Roger Lussier was kicking disconsolately at a tin can in the gutter, and Rollie Tremaine sat sullenly on the steps in front of the store.

"Save your money," Roger said. He had known about my plans to splurge on the cards.

"What's the matter?" I asked.

"There's no more cowboy cards," Rollie Tremaine said. "The company's not making any more."

"They're going to have president cards," Roger said, his face twisting with disgust. He pointed to the store window. "Look!"

A placard in the window announced: "Attention, Boys. Watch for the New Series. Presidents of the United States. Free in Each 5-Cent Package of Caramel Chew."

"President cards?" I asked, dismayed.

I read on: "Collect a Complete Set and Receive an Official Imitation Major League Baseball Glove, Embossed with Lefty Grove's Autograph."

Glove or no glove, who could become excited about presidents, of all things?

Rollie Tremaine stared at the sign. "Benjamin Harrison,

for crying out loud," he said. "Why would I want Benjamin
Harrison when I've got twenty-two Ken Maynards?"

I felt the warmth of guilt creep over me. I jingled the
coins in my pocket, but the sound was hollow. No more
Ken Maynards to buy.

"I'm going to buy a Mr. Goodbar," Rollie Tremaine
decided.

I was without appetite, indifferent even to a Baby Ruth,
which was my favorite. I thought of how I had betrayed
Armand and, worst of all, my father.

"I'll see you after supper," I called over my shoulder to
Roger as I hurried away toward home. I took the shortcut
behind the church, although it involved leaping over a tall
wooden fance, and I zigzagged recklessly through Mr.
Thibodeau's garden, trying to outrace my guilt. I pounded
up the steps and into the house, only to learn that Armand
had already taken Yolande and Yvette uptown to shop for
the birthday present.

I pedaled my bike furiously through the streets, ignoring the indignant horns of automobiles as I sliced through
the traffic. Finally I saw Armand and my sisters emerge
from the Monument Men's Shop. My heart sank when I
spied the long, slim package that Armand was holding.

"Did you buy the present yet?" I asked, although I knew
it was too late.

"Just now. A blue tie," Armand said. "What's the matter?"

"Nothing," I replied, my chest hurting.

He looked at me for a long moment. At first his eyes
were hard, but then they softened. He smiled at me, almost

sadly, and touched my arm. I turned away from him because I felt naked and exposed.

"It's all right," he said gently. "Maybe you've learned something." The words were gentle, but they held a curious dignity, the dignity remaining even when his voice suddenly cracked on the last syllable.

I wondered what was happening to me, because I did not know whether to laugh or cry.

Sister Angela was amazed when, a week before Christmas vacation, everybody in the class submitted a history essay worthy of a high mark—in some cases as high as A-minus. (Sister Angela did not believe that anyone in the world ever deserved an A.) She never learned—or at least she never let on that she knew—we all had become experts on the presidents because of the cards we purchased at Lemire's. Each card contained a picture of a president, and on the reverse side, a summary of his career. We looked at those cards so often that the biographies imprinted themselves on our minds without effort. Even our street-corner conversations were filled with such information as the fact that James Madison was called "The Father of the Constitution," or that John Adams had intended to become a minister.

The president cards were a roaring success and the cowboy cards were quickly forgotten. In the first place we did not receive gum with the cards, but a kind of chewy caramel. The caramel could be tucked into a corner of your mouth, bulging your cheek in much the same manner as wads of tobacco bulged the mouths of baseball stars. In the second place the competition for collecting the cards was fierce and frustrating—fierce because everyone was intent on being the first to send away for a baseball glove and frustrating because although there were only thirty-two presidents, including Franklin Delano Roosevelt, the variety at Lemire's was at a minimum. When the deliveryman left the boxes of cards at the store each Monday, we often discovered that one entire box was devoted to a single president—two weeks in a row the boxes contained nothing but Abraham Lincolns. One week Roger Lussier and I were the heroes of Frenchtown. We journeyed on our bicycles to the North Side, engaged three boys in a matching bout and returned with five new presidents, including Chester Alan Arthur, who up to that time had been missing.

Perhaps to sharpen our desire, the card company sent a sample glove to Mr. Lemire, and it dangled, orange and sleek, in the window. I was half sick with longing, thinking of my old glove at home, which I had inherited from Armand. But Rollie Tremaine's desire for the glove outdistanced my own. He even got Mr. Lemire to agree to give the glove in the window to the first person to get a complete set of cards, so that precious time wouldn't be wasted waiting for the postman.

We were delighted at Rollie Tremaine's frustration, especially since he was only a substitute player for the Tigers. Once after spending fifty cents on cards—all of which turned out to be Calvin Coolidge—he threw them to the ground, pulled some dollar bills out of his pocket and said, "The heck with it. I'm going to buy a glove!"

"Not that glove," Roger Lussier said. "Not a glove with

Lefty Grove's autograph. Look what it says at the bottom of the sign."

We all looked, although we knew the words by heart: "This Glove Is Not For Sale Anywhere."

Rollie Tremaine scrambled to pick up the cards from the sidewalk, pouting more than ever. After that he was quietly obsessed with the presidents, hugging the cards close to his chest and refusing to tell us how many more he needed to complete his set.

I too was obsessed with the cards, because they had become things of comfort in a world that had suddenly grown dismal. After Christmas a layoff at the shop had thrown my father out of work. He received no paycheck for four weeks, and the only income we had was from Armand's after-school job at the Blue and White Grocery Store—a job he lost finally when business dwindled as the layoff continued.

Although we had enough food and clothing—my father's credit had always been good, a matter of pride with him—the inactivity made my father restless and irritable. He did not drink any beer at all, and laughed loudly, but not convincingly, after gulping down a glass of water and saying, "Lent came early this year." The twins fell sick and went to the hospital to have their tonsils removed. My father was confident that he would return to work eventually and pay off his debts, but he seemed to age before our eyes.

When orders again were received at the comb shop and he returned to work, another disaster occurred, although I was the only one aware of it. Armand fell in love.

I discovered his situation by accident, when I happened

to pick up a piece of paper that had fallen to the floor in the bedroom he and I shared. I frowned at the paper, puzzled.

"Dear Sally, When I look into your eyes the world stands still . . ."

The letter was snatched from my hands before I finished reading it.

"What's the big idea, snooping around?" Armand asked, his face crimson. "Can't a guy have any privacy?"

He had never mentioned privacy before. "It was on the floor," I said. "I didn't know it was a letter. Who's Sally?"

He flung himself across the bed. "You tell anybody and I'll muckalize you," he threatened. "Sally Knowlton."

Nobody in Frenchtown had a name like Knowlton.

"A girl from the North Side?" I asked, incredulous.

He rolled over and faced me, anger in his eyes, and a kind of despair, too.

"What's the matter with that? Think she's too good for me?" he asked. "I'm warning you, Jerry, if you tell anybody . . ."

"Don't worry," I said. Love had no particular place in my life; it seemed an unnecessary waste of time. And a girl from the North Side was so remote that for all practical purposes she did not exist. But I was curious. "What are you writing her a letter for? Did she leave town, or something?"

"She hasn't left town," he answered. "I wasn't going to send it. I just felt like writing to her."

I was glad that I had never become involved with love— love that brought desperation to your eyes, that caused you to write letters you did not plan to send. Shrugging with indifference, I began to search in the closet for the old baseball glove. I found it on the shelf, under some old sneakers. The webbing was torn and the padding gone. I thought of the sting I would feel when a sharp grounder slapped into the glove, and I winced.

"You tell anybody about me and Sally and I'll—"

"I know. You'll muckalize me."

I did not divulge his secret and often shared his agony, particularly when he sat at the supper table and left my mother's special butterscotch pie untouched. I had never realized before how terrible love could be. But my compassion was short-lived because I had other things to worry about: report cards due at Eastertime; the loss of income from old Mrs. Belander, who had gone to live with a daughter in Boston; and, of course, the presidents.

Because a stalemate had been reached, the president cards were the dominant force in our lives—mine, Roger Lussier's and Rollie Tremaine's. For three weeks, as the baseball season approached, each of us had a complete set—complete except for one president, Grover Cleveland. Each time a box of cards arrived at the store we hurriedly bought them (as hurriedly as our funds allowed) and tore off the wrappers, only to be confronted by James Monroe or Martin Van Buren or someone else. But never Grover Cleveland, never the man who had been the twenty-second *and* the twenty-fourth president of the United States. We argued about Grover Cleveland. Should he be placed between Chester Alan Arthur and Benjamin Harrison as the twenty-second president or did he belong between Benjamin Harrison and William McKinley as the twenty-fourth president? Was the card company playing fair? Roger Lussier brought up a horrifying possibility—did we need *two* Grover Clevelands to complete the set?

Indignant, we stormed Lemire's and protested to the harassed storeowner, who had long since vowed never to stock a new series. Muttering angrily, he searched his bills and receipts for a list of rules.

"All right," he announced. "Says here you only need one Grover Cleveland to finish the set. Now get out, all of you, unless you've got money to spend."

Outside the store, Rollie Tremaine picked up an empty tobacco tin and scaled it across the street. "Boy," he said. "I'd give five dollars for a Grover Cleveland."

When I returned home I found Armand sitting on the piazza steps, his chin in his hands. His mood of dejection mirrored my own, and I sat down beside him. We did not say anything for a while.

"Want to throw the ball around?" I asked.

He sighed, not bothering to answer.

"You sick?" I asked.

He stood up and hitched up his trousers, pulled at his ear and finally told me what the matter was—there was a big dance next week at the high school, the Spring Promenade, and Sally had asked him to be her escort.

I shook my head at the folly of love. "Well, what's so bad about that?"

"How can I take Sally to a fancy dance?" he asked desperately. "I'd have to buy her a corsage ... And my shoes are practically falling apart. Pa's got too many worries now to buy me new shoes or give me money for flowers for a girl."

I nodded in sympathy. "Yeah," I said. "Look at me. Baseball time is almost here, and all I've got is that old glove. And no Grover Cleveland card yet . . ."

"Grover Cleveland?" he asked. "They've got some of those up on the North Side. Some kid was telling me there's a store that's got them. He says they're looking for Warren G. Harding."

"Holy smoke!" I said. "I've got an extra Warren G. Harding!" Pure joy sang in my veins. I ran to my bicycle, swung into the seat—and found that the front tire was flat.

"I'll help you fix it," Armand said.

Within half an hour I was at the North Side Drugstore, where several boys were matching cards on the sidewalk. Silently but blissfully I shouted: President Grover Cleveland, here I come!

After Armand had left for the dance, all dressed up as if it were Sunday, the small green box containing the corsage under his arm, I sat on the railing of the piazza, letting my feet dangle. The neighborhood was quiet because the French-town Tigers were at Daggett's Field, practicing for the first baseball game of the season.

I thought of Armand and the ridiculous expression on his face when he'd stood before the mirror in the bedroom. I'd avoided looking at his new black shoes. "Love," I muttered.

Spring had arrived in a sudden stampede of apple blossoms and fragrant breezes. Windows had been thrown open and dust mops had banged on the sills all day long as the women busied themselves with housecleaning. I was puzzled by my lethargy. Wasn't spring supposed to make everything bright and gay?

I turned at the sound of footsteps on the stairs. Roger Lussier greeted me with a sour face.

"I thought you were practicing with the Tigers," I said.

"Rollie Tremaine," he said. "I just couldn't stand him." He slammed his fist against the railing. "Jeez, why did *he* have to be the one to get a Grover Cleveland? You should see him showing off. He won't let anybody even touch that glove . . ."

I felt like Benedict Arnold and knew that I had to confess what I had done.

"Roger," I said, "I got a Grover Cleveland card up on the North Side. I sold it to Rollie Tremaine for five dollars."

"Are you crazy?" he asked.

"I needed that five dollars. It was an—an emergency."

"Boy!" he said, looking down at the ground and shaking his head. "What did you have to do a thing like that for?"

I watched him as he turned away and began walking down the stairs.

"Hey, Roger!" I called.

He squinted up at me as if I were a stranger, someone he'd never seen before.

"What?" he asked, his voice flat.

"I had to do it," I said. "Honest."

He didn't answer. He headed toward the fence, searching for the board we had loosened to give us a secret passage.

I thought of my father and Armand and Rollie Tremaine

and Grover Cleveland and wished that I could go away someplace far away. But there was no place to go.

Roger found the loose slat in the fance and slipped through. I felt betrayed: weren't you supposed to feel good when you did something fine and noble?

A moment later two hands gripped the top of the fence and Roger's face appeared. "Was it a real emergency?" he yelled.

"A real one!" I called. "Something important!"

His face dropped from sight and his voice reached me across the yard: "All right."

"See you tomorrow!" I yelled.

I swung my legs over the railing again. The gathering dusk began to soften the sharp edges of the fence, the roof-tops, the distant church steeple. I sat there a long time, waiting for the good feeling to come.

BUSINESS AT ELEVEN

Toshio Mori

When he came to our house one day and knocked on the door and immediately sold me a copy of *The Saturday Evening Post*, it was the beginning of our friendship and also the beginning of our business relationship.

His name is John. I call him Johnny and he is eleven. It is the age when he should be crazy about baseball or football or fishing. But he isn't. Instead he came again to our door and made a business proposition.

"I think you have many old magazines here," he said.

"Yes," I said, "I have magazines of all kinds in the basement."

"Will you let me see them?" he said.

"Sure," I said.

I took him down to the basement where the stacks of magazines stood in the corner. Immediately this little boy went over to the piles and lifted a number of magazines and examined the dates of each number and the names.

"Do you want to keep these?" he said.

"No. You can have them," I said.

"No. I don't want them for nothing," he said. "How much do you want for them?"

"You can have them for nothing," I said.

"No, I want to buy them," he said. "How much do you want for them?"

This was a boy of eleven, all seriousness and purpose.

"What are you going to do with the old magazines?"

"I am going to sell them to people," he said.

We arranged the financial matters satisfactorily. We agreed he was to pay three cents for each copy he took home. On the first day he took home an *Esquire*, a couple of old *Saturday Evening Posts*, a *Scribner's*, an *Atlantic Monthly*, and a *Collier's*. He said he would be back soon to buy more magazines.

When he came back several days later, I learned his name was John so I began calling him Johnny.

"How did you make out, Johnny?" I said.

"I sold them all," he said. "I made seventy cents altogether."

"Good for you," I said. "How do you manage to get seventy cents for old magazines?"

Johnny said as he made the rounds selling *The Saturday Evening Post*, he also asked the folks if there were any back numbers they particularly wanted. Sometimes, he said, people will pay unbelievable prices for copies they had missed and wanted very much to see some particular articles or pictures, or their favorite writers' stories.

"You are a smart boy," I said.

"Papa says, if I want to be a salesman, be a good salesman," Johnny said. "I'm going to be a good salesman."

"That's the way to talk," I said. "And what does your father do?"

"Dad doesn't do anything. He stays at home," Johnny said.

"Is he sick or something?" I said.

"No, he isn't sick," he said. "He's all right. There's nothing wrong with him."

"How long have you been selling *The Saturday Evening Post?*" I asked.

"Five years," he said. "I began at six."

"Your father is lucky to have a smart boy like you for a son," I said.

That day he took home a dozen or so of the old magazines. He said he had five standing orders, an *Esquire* issue of June 1937, *Atlantic Monthly* February 1938 number, a copy of December 11, 1937 issue of *The New Yorker*, *Story Magazine* of February 1934, and a *Collier's* of April 2, 1938. The others, he said, he was taking a chance at.

"I can sell them," Johnny said.

Several days later I saw Johnny again at the door.

"Hello, Johnny," I said. "Did you sell them already?"

"Not all," he said. "I have two left. But I want some more."

"All right," I said. "You must have good business."

"Yes," he said, "I am doing pretty good these days. I broke my own record selling *The Saturday Evening Post* this week."

"How much is that?" I said.

"I sold 167 copies this week," he said. "Most boys feel lucky if they sell seventy-five or one hundred copies. But not for me."

"How many are there in your family, Johnny?" I said.

"Six counting myself," he said. "There is my father, three smaller brothers, and two small sisters."

"Where's your mother?" I said.

"Mother died a year ago," Johnny said.

He stayed in the basement a good one hour sorting out the magazines he wished. I stood by and talked to him as he lifted each copy and inspected it thoroughly. When I asked him if he had made a good sale with the old magazines recently, he said yes. He sold the *Scribner's* Fiftieth Anniversary Issue for sixty cents. Then he said he made several good sales with *Esquire* and a *Vanity Fair* this week.

"You have a smart head, Johnny," I said. "You have found a new way to make money."

Johnny smiled and said nothing. Then he gathered up the fourteen copies he picked out and said he must be going now.

"Johnny," I said, "hereafter you pay two cents a copy. That will be enough."

Johnny looked at me.

"No," he said. "Three cents is all right. You must make a profit, too."

An eleven-year-old boy—I watched him go out with his short business-like stride.

Next day he was back early in the morning. "Back so soon?" I said.

"Yesterday's were all orders," he said. "I want some more today."

"You certainly have a good trade," I said.

"The people know me pretty good. And I know them pretty good," he said. And about ten minutes later he picked out seven copies and said that was all he was taking today.

"I am taking Dad shopping," he said. "I am going to buy a new hat and shoes for him today."

"He must be tickled," I said.

"You bet he is," Johnny said. "He told me to be sure and come home early."

So he said he was taking these seven copies to the customers who ordered them and then run home to get Dad.

Two days later Johnny wanted some more magazines. He said a Mr. Whitman who lived up a block wanted all the magazines with Theodore Dreiser's stories inside. Then he went on talking about other customers of his. Miss White, the schoolteacher, read Hemingway, and he said she would buy back copies with Hemingway stories anytime he brought them in. Some liked Sinclair Lewis, others Saroyan, Faulkner, Steinbeck, Mann, Faith Baldwin, Fannie Hurst, Thomas Wolfe. So it went. It was amazing how an eleven-year-old boy could remember the customers' preferences and not get mixed up.

One day I asked him what he wanted to do when he grew up. He said he wanted a book shop all his own. He said he would handle old books and old magazines as well as the new ones and own the biggest bookstore around the Bay Region.

"That is a good ambition," I said. "You can do it. Just keep up the good work and hold your customers."

On the same day, in the afternoon, he came around to the house holding several packages.

"This is for you," he said, handing over a package. "What is this?" I said.

Johnny laughed. "Open up and see for yourself," he said.

I opened it. It was a book rest, a simple affair but handy.

"I am giving these to all my customers," Johnny said.

"This is too expensive to give away, Johnny," I said. "You will lose all your profits."

"I picked them up cheap," he said. "I'm giving these away so the customers will remember me."

"That is right, too," I said. "You have good sense."

After that he came in about half a dozen times, each time taking with him ten or twelve copies of various magazines. He said he was doing swell. Also, he said he was now selling *Liberty* along with the *Saturday Evening Posts*.

Then for two straight weeks I did not see him once. I could not understand this. He had never missed coming to the house in two or three days. Something must be wrong, I thought. He must be sick, I thought.

One day I saw Johnny at the door. "Hello, Johnny," I said. "Where were you? Were you sick?"

"No. I wasn't sick," Johnny said.

"What's the matter? What happened?" I said.

"I'm moving away," Johnny said. "My father is moving to Los Angeles."

"Sit down, Johnny," I said. "Tell me all about it."

He sat down. He told me what had happened in two weeks. He said his dad went and got married to a woman he, Johnny, did not know. And now, his dad and this woman say they are moving to Los Angeles. And about all there was for him to do was to go along with them.

"I don't know what to say, Johnny," I said.

Johnny said nothing. We sat quietly and watched the time move.

"Too bad you will lose your good trade," I finally said.

"Yes. I know," he said. "But I can sell magazines in Los Angeles."

"Yes, that is true," I said.

Then he said he must be going. I wished him good luck. We shook hands. "I will come and see you again," he said.

"And when I visit Los Angeles some day," I said, "I will see you in the largest bookstore in the city."

Johnny smiled. As he walked away, up the street and out of sight, I saw the last of him walking like a good businessman, walking briskly, energetically, purposefully.

LA CIRAMELLA

Mary K. Mazotti

Nothing in the house to do?" I heard Papa say as I sat reading on the steps of the front porch. He towered before me like a yellow giant. Papa had just finished sulfuring our vineyard across the dirt road and was covered with the yellow powder.

"We did everything you told us, Papa," I answered, speaking for my two younger sisters and myself. He grunted with satisfaction. Idle daughters always set him on edge, as busyness was Papa's way of life. He turned and walked slowly to the faucet trough to wash up for our main meal of the day. I carefully pinched a rose leaf from the trellis to make a book mark and scooted inside to set the table. It was a spring Saturday, 1936, and six long years into the Depression.

Each early spring the sun's bright rising was directly over our vineyard and small house. In spite of the Depression Mama saw the wand of golden rays as a blessing for her and Papa, and their three young daughters born in America. Times in America could never match the poverty of their native rocky villages in southern Italy. And Mama never stopped pouring out words of gratitude for finding a better life.

Papa was famished from spraying sulfur all morning. Now he seemed content that the new grapes were protected from mildew. He sniffed the homemade noodles Mama had prepared.

"Una festa!" he spoke through his nostrils. Mama had tossed the noodles with hot olive oil, minced garlic, and fresh basil, and sprinkled over them her grated goat cheese.

"Pronto," Mama said, putting the steaming platter carefully on the round oak table. Making a swift blessing over our food, Mama served everyone.

I watched Mama's flushed cheeks as she ate. I knew she was hungry. Early that morning she had heated tubs of water on a fire pit outside to wash clothes. She stood stooped for hours scrubbing bed sheets and towels on the scrub board, twisting and twisting out suds and rinse water, and then pinning them to wire lines strung on the sunny side of the house, where carnations and hollyhocks bloomed.

Needless to say, I and my sisters, Lomena and Pina, felt hunger rumbles also from doing housework and picking up around the big yard like Papa told us to do.

Papa finished the first dish of noodles and was into his second when he got off on a conversation about how life used to be in his native village of Grisolia where he was born. (Papa and Mama often spoke of their little villages. Mama spoke of San Sosti.) I tried hard to picture it all and liked to share these stories with my sixth-grade teacher, whom I adored and respected. Papa became very nostalgic as he recalled the fun things that happened as he grew up in Grisolia.

"The thing I itch to do most," he said, "is to play a *ciramella* again." My sisters and I stared blankly.

Mama explained, "It's a music instrument—a bagpipe, made of goatskin."

Lomena and Pina giggled. Staring at my father's unshaven face, I scowled, "Goatskin!" What a stinky instrument, I was about to blurt out, but I knew better than to make fun of my father.

Papa rushed on, his face rosy, "I tell you, no one could play the goatskin like me." Laying down his fork rolled fat with noodles, he pretended playing one. With both hands uplifted, he made droning bagpipe sounds come from his nose by wrinkling it upward and humming through his teeth.

This time I laughed till the tears came. "I didn't know you were a musician, Papa," I said with amazement.

"By the saints!" he answered. "I think I'll just make one for old-time sake. It will take the place of the one I left behind in Grisolia. What a pity I was talked out of bringing it to America by *cara* Mama. I let her load me up with dried sausage and her bread instead."

My mother stopped eating. She pushed a loose hairpin into her hair bun. "*Ma*, Nichole," she teased, "what do you know about bagpipe making?" Flinging her right hand upward, she went on, "When was the last time you've seen one?"

Papa stuck out his chin and huffed, "Elena, I can remember a sack of things! What is needed? What is needed?" he repeated, and answered for himself, "Just the skin of a young goat and pipes for playing. That's all!"

"*Sì, Sì*," Mama argued back, with twinkling eyes and still teasing. "What little I remember the skin has to be peeled off carefully—like a sock, not slit down the middle—to make an airtight bag. And curing the skin! It's not something simple, like swatting flies."

Papa couldn't help but laugh. He liked Mama's sharp sense of humor. He then got up to take some food scraps to Primo, his dog, without saying more about the matter. I wondered, as my sister Lomena and I washed the dishes in a pan of hot water, if Papa would really make a *ciramella*.

My mother and father had met and wed in their new country of America, in the early 1920s, when thousands of Italians left families behind and sailed across oceans to find better lives in new lands. They settled in California, in the San Joaquin Valley, where young vineyards, orchards, and farmlands and small shops were already started by friends before them, and by Armenians, Greeks, Mexicans, and French.

Now, in 1936, America was still having bad times called a Depression. People were out of work. Banks were failing and families lost home and hard-worked lands because they couldn't make payments. Worse, crops were not paying much.

Papa and Mama already knew how to make do with little. Fortunately, Papa had his land free of debt before he married Mama. And Nonna, Mama's mother, let them live in the small two-bedroom house rent-free when she moved to San Francisco. There were plenty of fruit trees and vegetables Papa had planted across the road; eggs from hens, milk from the goat, and catches of rabbits and quails by Papa. Sacks of flour and gallons of cooking oil were bought with side-job money Papa made on other ranches. And Papa was never without a bottle of homemade wine from his own vineyard to help his digestion, and to help him relax from long hours of work.

One evening the whole family walked to the east side of Clovis to visit Papa's *paesano*, Carlo, and family. Carlo and his wife, Amelia, were godparents to Lomena and me. They had a family of twelve children. I liked to visit them because their oldest daughter, Theresa, and I were good friends. We liked to giggle and talk about friends and growing up.

I had forgotten all about Papa making the bagpipe until I overheard him bring up old times in Italy to my godfather. Papa didn't say he was going to make a bagpipe; he just asked clever questions about how to make one. I thought, How wise Papa is. He still dreamed of making one, but wanted to save embarrassment if it didn't turn out right. After our visit, my godfather took us home in his old Studebaker.

As he did every springtime, Papa bought a young goat

from a farmer. Besides giving the family rest from eating jackrabbits and chicken meat, the goat provided the skin for the *ciramella*. I was glad that we were in school when Papa did the butchering and skinning behind the chicken shed. Only Primo, the dog, watched. Papa got the dog from a friend and named him after Primo Carnera, an Italian world heavyweight champion boxer a few years back.

Papa had removed the skin as he wanted it—whole, except with openings at top and bottom, and where the legs stood. Then followed many weeks of scraping off the hair, and rubbing and soaking the skin to make it soft.

One day Mama complained to Papa, "*Mamma mia!* What strange things I'm putting up with these days, Nichole. You have used my washtubs to treat your *ciramella* skin and my clothes are drying an ugly smell."

"I didn't know," said Papa. "*Basta.* That's it. I'm finished with the treatments. I'll scour the tubs with wood ashes for you—that is, if you write a letter for me."

Mama pulled her black-and-white-checkered apron above her plump middle and said, "Let me guess. You want me to write to your father in Italy for the blowpipe and sounding pipes for the *ciramella.*"

"Please," said Papa, "you know how poor my writing is." So Mama did. I was proud that she had learned to write in Italian before she came to America. She even went to school in America up to the fourth grade. Papa was still struggling with his writing, and I was amazed at how fancy he could write when he made up his mind.

Every night my father pinned the bagpipe skin to the clothesline to air out. Not long after, he was heard yelling,

"What happened to it? What's happened to it?" We all dashed outside. Papa was red with anger. The line was broken and the skin gone. Everyone searched at least three times, every spot of the yard. Just when the skin seemed forever lost, Papa looked in Primo's doghouse. There it was next to him. Papa shook his fist and cursed. Primo ran and hid behind the woodpile. But I knew it wasn't Primo's fault the clothesline broke.

Late October when grape leaves had turned yellow, and some purple red, and the grapes were picked, Papa brought home a package from the post office. "They have arrived," he said happily tearing open the package. Lomena and I jumped up from doing our homework and Pina from her scribbling.

"Can we watch, Papa?" Pina said, jumping up and down. "Sure, Little Squash," answered Papa as he unwrapped the brown pipes. "And after we eat, I'll fit them into the skin."

That afternoon I carried in cut grape stumps to warm up the kitchen. The stumps threw off good heat to warm up the neat tiny living room, two bedrooms, and large, kitchen-eating area. Papa worked on a bench that we kept for company. As Mama toasted fava beans for munching, he marked the skin leg opening that would be used to fit in the blowpipe and valve. He fitted the sounding pipes in the neck opening and bound them in place tightly with twisted hemp. Papa neatly sewed up the bottom and remaining leg openings.

"It looks like a giant flat pear with horns," I whispered softly in Lomena's ear. She bent over with laughter.

"What's next, Papa?" said Pina, pulling on the elastic of the flannel pajamas Mama had made her.

"Air," said Papa. "Lots of it." He blew and blew into the bagpipe and rested. Then he blew until the bag got fat. He put his fingers on some piping holes and let air gush out of the others. Wails and squeaks filled the kitchen. I ran to the bedroom to hide my laughter. Lomena followed.

"What terrible music," she gasped, laughing and holding her side.

"Shhh, not so loud," I warned. "Papa will think we are disrespectful."

Before supper, each day, Papa went down to the cellar, pulled on the overhead light string, pulled down the double doors, and practiced on his *ciramella*. He played the old tunes of the old country until they came out like he wanted them to. Within days *paesanos* and friends knew there was a *ciramella* in the Bono household.

"Yes, yes," Papa admitted, "I have made a *ciramella*."

"Well, play for us," they begged.

"At Christmastime," Papa promised. So he kept them waiting until then.

School was out for Christmas vacation. My sisters and I took turns wheeling chopped wood to the kitchen door for Mama's baking. First she made the wine and honey cookies and fig bars drizzled with white frosting; then came the pretzel-shaped bread sticks with anise seeds; finally, the fried dough puffs stuffed with preserved sardines and dried red peppers that had been soaked in boiling water. Mama hummed and sang Christmas songs along with the old Philco radio in the living room.

Lomena and I made fringed napkins from the bleached flour sacks as gifts for Mama. Lomena drew sweet little violets on a corner of each napkin and we embroidered six napkins each.

The time was right for Papa. He visited friends and personally invited them for a night of *ciramella* music and Christmas joy. We decorated the living room ceiling with chains of red and green construction paper. A small red candle was lit and placed by the picture of the Christ Child upon Mama's treadle sewing machine. The bare floors had been mopped clean earlier in the day by Mama.

That evening lights shone in every room of our house. They glowed a long ways down the road. Friends with their children walked or drove up in their secondhand cars. The December air stung noses and ears as bright as stars speckled the valley heavens. Our walls shook with laughter and chattering.

"Nichole, come on now! How much longer do we have to wait to hear your *ciramella?*" hollered Rocco, who had left the old country with Papa.

"*Sì*, Nichole, let's see this secret project you kept from us for so long," begged Pietro, the bachelor.

Papa brought in the *ciramella* from the screened-in porch. He held it high over his head for all to see.

"It's just like the ones in the old country," marveled my godmother, Amelia.

"*Sì, sì*," they all agreed. "Exactly!"

The men enjoyed sipping Papa's best wine and took turns blowing air into the bagpipe, laughing all the while as it grew fatter and fatter.

Then Papa took his *ciramella*. As he blew through the bagpipe, his fingers moved over the piping holes. Gentle wailing sounds became folk melodies of a long-ago homeland. Men and women sang songs they learned before they ever dreamed of seeing America. Tears slid down their cheeks and it became hard for them to sing.

Suddenly Papa stopped playing. "*Basta!* Enough crying!" he shouted. "We are not at a funeral parlor. We are in America! Time to be glad. Time to dance!" He began playing one tarantella after another. Women spread wide their skirts and danced around their husbands—back and forth, hands on hips, round and round each other they danced. Children found partners and did the same in corners, copying.

"*Bravo*, Niccolò! *Bravo!*" friends yelled.

That night Papa appeared to me as one gigantic happy glow. I wanted the night never to end.

Winter passed and then spring. As summer moved into July, a heat wave hit the valley. A terrible odor began to hang in the house.

Lomena complained loudly, "Mama, my stomach wants to throw up from the smell."

Papa sniffed his way to a shelf in the screened-in porch. "*Dio!*" he groaned. "Can it be—no, it can't be!"

"I think your bagpipe is beginning to rot inside," said Mama, holding her nose.

"What a waste," said Papa. "We could have had more fun with it."

We felt sad for Papa. Who could ever forget that Christmas night? Without another word, Papa ripped out the pipes from the *ciramella* and took the skin to the backyard. He grabbed the shovel standing upright in the dirt by the water faucet and dug a deep hole. He plopped in the skin and filled up the hole, stomping on the dirt with his shoes to seal in the odor. I watched as Papa put the shovel back where it stood before; without looking up, he strode across the road and into the vineyard.

THE WHITE UMBRELLA

Gish Jen

When I was twelve, my mother went to work without telling me or my little sister.

"Not that we need the second income." The lilt of her accent drifted from the kitchen up to the top of the stairs, where Mona and I were listening.

"No," said my father, in a barely audible voice. "Not like the Lee family."

The Lees were the only other Chinese family in town. I remembered how sorry my parents had felt for Mrs. Lee when she started waitressing downtown the year before; and so when my mother began coming home late, I didn't say anything, and tried to keep Mona from saying anything either.

"But why shouldn't I?" she argued. "Lots of people's mothers work."

"Those are American people," I said.

"So what do you think we are? I can do the Pledge of Allegiance with my eyes closed."

Nevertheless, she tried to be discreet; and if my mother wasn't home by 5:30, we would start cooking by ourselves, to make sure dinner would be on time. Mona would wash the vegetables and put on the rice; I would chop.

For weeks we wondered what kind of work she was doing. I imagined that she was selling perfume, testing dessert recipes for the local newspaper. Or maybe she was working for the florist. Now that she had learned to drive, she might be delivering boxes of roses to people.

"I don't think so," said Mona as we walked to our piano lesson after school. "She would've hit something by now."

A gust of wind littered the street with leaves.

"Maybe we better hurry up," she went on, looking at the sky. "It's going to pour."

"But we're too early." Her lesson didn't begin until 4:00, mine until 4:30, so we usually tried to walk as slowly as we could. "And anyway, those aren't the kind of clouds that rain. Those are cumulus clouds."

We arrived out of breath and wet.

"Oh, you poor, poor dears," said old Miss Crosman. "Why don't you call me the next time it's like this out? If your mother won't drive you, I can come pick you up."

"No, that's okay," I answered. Mona wrung her hair out on Miss Crosman's rug. "We just couldn't get the roof of our car to close, is all. We took it to the beach last summer and got sand in the mechanism." I pronounced this last word carefully, as if the credibility of my lie depended on its middle syllable. "It's never been the same." I thought for a second. "It's a convertible."

"Well then make yourselves at home." She exchanged looks with Eugenie Roberts, whose lesson we were interrupting. Eugenie smiled good-naturedly. "The towels are in the closet across from the bathroom."

Huddling at the end of Miss Crosman's nine-foot leatherette couch, Mona and I watched Eugenie play. She was a grade ahead of me and, according to school rumor, had a boyfriend in high school. I believed it. Aside from her ballooning breasts—which threatened to collide with the keyboard as she played—she had auburn hair, blue eyes, and, I noted with a particular pang, a pure white, folding umbrella.

"I can't see," whispered Mona.

"So clean your glasses."

"My glasses *are* clean. You're in the way."

I looked at her. "They look dirty to me."

"That's because *your* glasses are dirty."

Eugenie came bouncing to the end of her piece.

"Oh! Just stupendous!" Miss Crosman hugged her, then looked up as Eugenie's mother walked in. "Stupendous!" she said again. "Oh! Mrs. Roberts! Your daughter has a gift, a real gift. It's an honor to teach her."

Mrs. Roberts, radiant with pride, swept her daughter out of the room as if she were royalty, born to the piano bench. Watching the way Eugenie carried herself, I sat up, and concentrated so hard on sucking in my stomach that I did not realize until the Robertses were gone that Eugenie had left her umbrella. As Mona began to play, I jumped up and ran to the window, meaning to call to them—only to see their brake lights flash then fade at the stop sign at the corner. As if to allow them passage, the rain had let up; a quivering sun lit their way.

The umbrella glowed like a scepter on the blue carpet while Mona, slumping over the keyboard, managed to eke out a fair rendition of a catfight. At the end of the piece, Miss Crosman asked her to stand up.

"Stay right there," she said, then came back a minute later with a towel to cover the bench. "You must be cold," she continued. "Shall I call your mother and have her bring over some dry clothes?"

"No," answered Mona. "She won't come because she . . ."

"She's too busy," I broke in from the back of the room.

"I see." Miss Crosman sighed and shook her head a little. "Your glasses are filthy, honey," she said to Mona. "Shall I clean them for you?"

Sisterly embarrassment seized me. Why hadn't Mona wiped her lenses when I told her to? As she resumed abuse of the piano, I stared at the umbrella. I wanted to open it, twirl it around by its slender silver handle; I wanted to dangle it from my wrist on the way to school the way the other girls did. I wondered what Miss Crosman would say if I offered to bring it to Eugenie at school tomorrow. She would be impressed with my consideration for others; Eugenie would be pleased to have it back; and I would have possession of the umbrella for an entire night. I looked at it again, toying with the idea of asking for one for Christmas. I knew, however, how my mother would react.

"Things," she would say. "What's the matter with a raincoat? All you want is things, just like an American."

Sitting down for my lesson, I was careful to keep the towel under me and sit up straight.

"I'll bet you can't see a thing either," said Miss Crosman, reaching for my glasses. "And you can relax, you poor dear." She touched my chest, in an area where she never would have touched Eugenie Roberts. "This isn't a boot camp."

When Miss Crosman finally allowed me to start playing I played extra well, as well as I possibly could. See, I told her with my fingers. You don't have to feel sorry for me.

"That was wonderful," said Miss Crosman. "Oh! Just wonderful."

An entire constellation rose in my heart.

"And guess what," I announced proudly. "I have a surprise for you."

Then I played a second piece for her, a much more difficult one that she had not assigned.

"Oh! That was stupendous," she said without hugging me. "Stupendous! You are a genius, young lady. If your mother had started you younger, you'd be playing like Eugenie Roberts by now!"

I looked at the keyboard, wishing that I had still a third, even more difficult piece to play for her. I wanted to tell her that I was the school spelling bee champion, that I wasn't ticklish, that I could do karate.

"My mother is a concert pianist," I said.

She looked at me for a long moment, then finally, without saying anything, hugged me. I didn't say anything about bringing the umbrella to Eugenie at school.

The steps were dry when Mona and I sat down to wait for my mother.

"Do you want to wait inside?" Miss Crosman looked anxiously at the sky.

"No," I said. "Our mother will be here any minute."

"In a while," said Mona.

"Any minute," I said again, even though my mother had been at least twenty minutes late every week since she started working.

According to the church clock across the street we had been waiting twenty-five minutes when Miss Crosman came out again.

"Shall I give you ladies a ride home?"

"No," I said. "Our mother is coming any minute."

"Shall I at least give her a call and remind her you're here? Maybe she forgot about you."

"I don't think she *forgot*," said Mona.

"Shall I give her a call anyway? Just to be safe?"

"I bet she already left," I said. "How could she forget about us?"

Miss Crosman went in to call.

"There's no answer," she said, coming back out.

"See, she's on her way," I said.

"Are you sure you wouldn't like to come in?"

"No," said Mona.

"Yes," I said. I pointed at my sister. "She meant yes, too. She meant no, she wouldn't like to go in."

Miss Crosman looked at her watch. "It's 5:30 now, ladies. My pot roast will be coming out in fifteen minutes. Maybe you'd like to come in and have some then?"

"My mother's almost here," I said. "She's on her way."

We watched and watched the street. I tried to imagine what my mother was doing; I tried to imagine her writing messages in the sky, even though I knew she was afraid of planes. I watched as the branches of Miss Crosman's big willow tree started to sway; they had all been trimmed to exactly the same height off the ground, so that they looked beautiful, like hair in the wind.

It started to rain.

"Miss Crosman is coming out again," said Mona.

"Don't let her talk you into going inside," I whispered.

"Why not?"

"Because that would mean Mom isn't really coming any minute."

"But she isn't," said Mona. "She's *working*."

"Shhh! Miss Crosman is going to hear you."

"She's working! She's working! She's working!"

I put my hand over her mouth, but she licked it, and so I was wiping my hand on my wet dress when the front door opened.

"We're getting even *wetter*," said Mona right away. "Wetter and wetter."

"Shall we all go in?" Miss Crosman pulled Mona to her feet. "Before you young ladies catch pneumonia? You've been out here an hour already."

"We're *freezing*." Mona looked up at Miss Crosman. "Do you have any hot chocolate? We're going to catch *pneumonia*."

"I'm not going in," I said. "My mother's coming any minute."

"Come on," said Mona. "Use your *noggin*."

"Any minute."

"Come on, Mona," Miss Crosman opened the door. Shall we get you inside first?"

"See you in the hospital," said Mona as she went in. "See you in the hospital with *pneumonia*."

I stared out into the empty street. The rain was pricking me all over; I was cold; I wanted to go inside. I wanted to be able to let myself go inside. If Miss Crosman came out again, I decided, I would go in.

She came out with a blanket and the white umbrella.

I could not believe that I was actually holding the umbrella, opening it. It sprang up by itself as if it were alive, as if that were what it wanted to do—as if it belonged in my hands, above my head. I stared up at the network of silver spokes, then spun the umbrella around and around and around. It was so clean and white that it seemed to glow, to illuminate everything around it.

"It's beautiful," I said.

Miss Crosman sat down next to me, on one end of the blanket. I moved the umbrella over so that it covered that too. I could feel the rain on my left shoulder and shivered. She put her arm around me.

"You poor, poor dear."

I knew that I was in store for another bolt of sympathy, and braced myself by staring up into the umbrella.

"You know, I very much wanted to have children when I was younger," she continued.

"You did?"

She stared at me a minute. Her face looked dry and crusty, like day-old frosting.

"I did. But then I never got married."

I twirled the umbrella around again.

"This is the most beautiful umbrella I have ever seen," I said. "Ever, in my whole life."

"Do you have an umbrella?"

"No. But my mother's going to get me one just like this for Christmas."

"Is she? I tell you what. You don't have to wait until Christmas. You can have this one."

"But this one belongs to Eugenie Roberts," I protested. "I have to give it back to her tomorrow in school."

"Who told you it belongs to Eugenie? It's not Eugenie's. It's mine. And now I'm giving it to you, so it's yours."

"It is?"

She hugged me tighter. "That's right. It's all yours."

"It's mine?" I didn't know what to say. "Mine?" Suddenly I was jumping up and down in the rain. "It's beautiful! Oh! It's beautiful!" I laughed.

Miss Crosman laughed, too, even though she was getting all wet.

"Thank you, Miss Crosman. Thank you very much. Thanks a zillion. It's beautiful. It's *stupendous*!"

"You're quite welcome," she said.

"Thank you," I said again, but that didn't seem like enough. Suddenly I knew just what she wanted to hear. "I wish you were my mother."

Right away I felt bad.

"You shouldn't say that," she said, but her face was opening into a huge smile as the lights of my mother's car cautiously turned the corner. I quickly collapsed the umbrella and put it up my skirt, holding onto it from the outside, through the material.

"Mona!" I shouted into the house. "Mona! Hurry up! Mom's here! I told you she was coming!"

Then I ran away from Miss Crosman, down to the curb. Mona came tearing up to my side as my mother neared the house. We both backed up a few feet, so that in case she went onto the curb, she wouldn't run us over.

"But why didn't you go inside with Mona!" my mother asked on the way home. She had taken off her own coat to put over me, and had the heat on high.

"She wasn't using her noggin," said Mona, next to me in the back seat.

"I should call next time," said my mother. "I just don't like to say where I am."

That was when she finally told us that she was working as a check-out clerk in the A&P. She was supposed to be on the day shift, but the other employees were unreliable, and her boss had promised her a promotion if she would stay until the evening shift filled in.

For a moment no one said anything. Even Mona seemed to find the revelation disappointing.

"A promotion already!" she said, finally.

I listened to the windshield wipers.

"You're so quiet." My mother looked at me in the rear-view mirror. "What's the matter?"

"I wish you would quit," I said after a moment.

She sighed. "The Chinese have a saying: one beam cannot hold the roof up."

"But Eugenie Roberts's father supports their family."

She signed once more. "Eugenie Roberts's father is Eugenie Roberts's father," she said.

As we entered the downtown area, Mona started leaning hard against me every time the car turned right, trying to push me over. Remembering what I had said to Miss Crosman, I tried to maneuver the umbrella under my leg so she wouldn't feel it.

"What's under your skirt?" Mona wanted to know as we came to a traffic light. My mother, watching us in the rearview mirror again, rolled slowly to a stop.

"What's the matter?" she asked.

"There's something under her skirt?" said Mona, pulling at me. "Under her skirt?"

Meanwhile, a man crossing the street started to yell at us. "Who do you think you are, lady?" he said. "You're blocking the whole damn crosswalk."

We all froze. Other people walking by stopped to watch.

"Didn't you hear me?" he went on, starting to thump on the hood with his fist. "Don't you speak English?"

My mother began to back up, but the car behind us honked. Luckily, the light turned green right after that. She sighed in relief.

"What were you saying, Mona?" she asked.

We wouldn't have hit the car behind us that hard if he hadn't been moving, too, but as it was our car bucked violently, throwing us all first back and then forward.

"Uh oh," said Mona when we stopped. "*Another* accident."

I was relieved to have attention diverted from the umbrella. Then I noticed my mother's head, tilted back onto the seat. Her eyes were closed.

"Mom!" I screamed. "Mom! Wake up!"

She opened her eyes. "Please don't yell," she said. "Enough people are going to yell already."

"I thought you were dead," I said, starting to cry. "I thought you were dead."

She turned around, looked at me intently, then put her hand to my forehead.

"Sick," she confirmed. "Some kind of sick is giving you crazy ideas."

As the man from the car behind us started tapping on the window, I moved the umbrella away from my leg. Then Mona and my mother were getting out of the car. I got out after them; and while everyone else was inspecting the damage we'd done, I threw the umbrella down a sewer.

HAMADI

Naomi Shihab Nye

---

*"It takes two of us to discover truth: one to utter it and
one to understand it."*

KAHLIL GIBRAN, *Sand and Foam*

Susan didn't really feel interested in Saleh Hamadi until
she was a freshman in high school carrying a thousand
questions around. Why this way? Why not another way?
Who said so and why can't I say something else? Those
brittle women at school in the counselor's office treated the
world as if it were a yardstick and they had tight hold of
both ends.

Sometimes Susan felt polite with them, sorting attendance cards during her free period, listening to them gab
about fingernail polish and television. And other times she
felt she could run out of the building yelling. That's when
she daydreamed about Saleh Hamadi, who had nothing to

do with any of it. Maybe she thought of him as escape, the
way she used to think about the Sphinx at Giza when she
was younger. She would picture the golden Sphinx sitting
quietly in the desert with sand blowing around its face,
never changing its expression. She would think of its wry,
slightly crooked mouth and how her grandmother looked
a little like that as she waited for her bread to bake in the
old village north of Jerusalem. Susan's family had lived in
Jerusalem for three years before she was ten and drove out
to see her grandmother every weekend. They would find
her patting fresh dough between her hands, or pressing
cakes of dough onto the black rocks in the *taboon*, the
rounded old oven outdoors. Sometimes she moved her lips
as she worked. Was she praying? Singing a secret song?
Susan had never seen her grandmother rushing.

Now that she was fourteen, she took long walks in
America with her father down by the drainage ditch at the
end of their street. Pecan trees shaded the path. She tried
to get him to tell stories about his childhood in Palestine.
She didn't want him to forget anything. She helped her
American mother complete tedious kitchen tasks without
complaining—rolling grape leaves around their lemony rice
stuffing, scrubbing carrots for the roaring juicer. Some evenings when the soft Texas twilight pulled them all outside,
she thought of her far-away grandmother and said, "Let's
go see Saleh Hamadi. Wouldn't he like some of that cheese
pie Mom made?" And they would wrap a slice of pie and
drive downtown. Somehow he felt like a good substitute
for a grandmother, even though he was a man.

Usually Hamadi was wearing a white shirt, shiny black

tie, and a jacket that reminded Susan of the earth's surface just above the treeline on a mountain—thin, somehow purified. He would raise his hands high before giving advice.

"It is good to drink a tall glass of water every morning upon arising!" If anyone doubted this, he would shake his head. "Oh Susan, Susan, Susan," he would say.

He did not like to sit down, but he wanted everyone else to sit down. He made Susan sit on the wobbly chair beside the desk and he made her father or mother sit in the saggy center of the bed. He told them people should eat six small meals a day.

They visited him on the sixth floor of the Traveler's Hotel, where he had lived so long nobody could remember him ever traveling. Susan's father used to remind him of the apartments available over the Victory Cleaners, next to the park with the fizzy pink fountain, but Hamadi would shake his head, pinching kisses at his spartan room. "A white handkerchief spread across a tabletop, my two extra shoes lined by the wall, this spells 'home' to me, this says 'mi casa.' What more do I need?"

Hamadi liked to use Spanish words. They made him feel expansive, worldly. He'd learned them when he worked at the fruits and vegetables warehouse on Zarzamora Street, marking off crates of apples and avocados on a long white pad. Occasionally he would speak Arabic, his own first language, with Susan's father and uncles, but he said it made him feel too sad, as if his mother might step into the room at any minute, her arms laden with fresh mint leaves. He had come to the United States on a boat when he was eighteen years old and he had never been married. "I married books," he said. "I married the wide horizon."

"What is he to us?" Susan used to ask her father. "He's not a relative, right? How did we meet him to begin with?"

Susan's father couldn't remember. "I think we just drifted together. Maybe we met at your uncle Hani's house. Maybe that old Maronite priest who used to cry after every service introduced us. The priest once shared an apartment with Kahlil Gibran in New York—so he said. And Saleh always says he stayed with Gibran when he first got off the boat. I'll bet that popular guy Gibran has had a lot of roommates he doesn't even know about."

Susan said, "Dad, he's dead."

"I know, I know," her father said.

Later Susan said, "Mr. Hamadi, did you really meet Kahlil Gibran? He's one of my favorite writers." Hamadi walked slowly to the window of his room and stared out. There wasn't much to look at down on the street—a bedraggled flower shop, a boarded-up tavern with a hand-lettered sign tacked to the front, GONE TO FIND JESUS. Susan's father said the owners had really gone to Alabama.

Hamadi spoke patiently. "Yes, I met brother Gibran. And I meet him in my heart every day. When I was a young man—shocked by all the visions of the new world—the tall buildings—the wild traffic—the young people without shame—the proud mailboxes in their blue uniforms—I met him. And he has stayed with me every day of my life."

"But did you really meet him, like in person, or just in a book?"

He turned dramatically. "Make no such distinctions, my friend. Or your life will be a pod with only dried-up beans inside. Believe anything can happen."

Susan's father looked irritated, but Susan smiled. "I do," she said. "I believe that. I want fat beans. If I imagine something, it's true, too. Just a different kind of true."

Susan's father was twiddling with the knobs on the old-fashioned sink. "Don't they even give you hot water here? You don't mean to tell me you've been living without hot water?"

On Hamadi's rickety desk lay a row of different "Love" stamps issued by the post office.

"You must write a lot of letters," Susan said.

"No, no, I'm just focusing on that word," Hamadi said. "I particularly like the globe in the shape of a heart," he added.

"Why don't you take a trip back to your village in Lebanon?" Susan's father asked. "Maybe you still have relatives living there."

Hamadi looked pained. " 'Remembrance is a form of meeting,' my brother Gibran says, and I do believe I meet with my cousins every day."

"But aren't you curious? You've been gone so long! Wouldn't you like to find out what has happened to everybody and everything you knew as a boy?" Susan's father traveled back to Jerusalem once each year to see his family.

"I would not. In fact, I already know. It is there and it is not there. Would you like to share an orange with me?"

His long fingers, tenderly peeling. Once when Susan

was younger, he'd given her a lavish ribbon off a holiday fruit basket and expected her to wear it on her head. In the car, Susan's father said, "Riddles. He talks in riddles. I don't know why I have patience with him." Susan stared at the people talking and laughing in the next car. She did not even exist in their world.

Susan carried *The Prophet* around on top of her English textbook and her Texas history. She and her friend Tracy read it out loud to one another at lunch. Tracy was a junior— they'd met at the literary magazine meeting where Susan, the only freshman on the staff, got assigned to do proofreading. They never ate in the cafeteria; they sat outside at picnic tables with sack lunches, whole wheat crackers and fresh peaches. Both of them had given up meat.

Tracy's eyes looked steamy. "You know that place where Gibran says, 'Hate is a dead thing. Who of you would be a tomb?'"

Susan nodded. Tracy continued. "Well, I hate someone. I'm trying not to, but I can't help it. I hate Debbie for liking Eddie and it's driving me nuts."

"Why shouldn't Debbie like Eddie?" Susan said. "*You* do."

Tracy put her head down on her arms. A gang of cheerleaders walked by giggling. One of them flicked her finger in greeting.

"In fact, we *all* like Eddie," Susan said. "Remember, here in this book—wait and I'll find it—where Gibran says that loving teaches us the secrets of our hearts and that's the way we connect to all of Life's heart? You're not talking about liking or loving, you're talking about owning."

Tracy looked glum. "Sometimes you remind me of a minister."

Susan said, "Well, just talk to me someday when *I'm* depressed."

Susan didn't want a boyfriend. Everyone who had boyfriends or girlfriends seemed to have troubles. Susan told people she had a boyfriend far away, on a farm in Missouri, but the truth was, boys still seemed like cousins to her. Or brothers. Or even girls.

A squirrel sat in the crook of a tree, eyeing their sandwiches. When the end-of-lunch bell blared, Susan and Tracy jumped—it always seemed too soon. Squirrels were lucky; they didn't have to go to school.

Susan's father said her idea was ridiculous: to invite Saleh Hamadi to go Christmas caroling with the English Club. "His English is archaic, for one thing, and he won't know *any* of the songs."

"How could you live in America for years and not know 'Joy to the World' or 'Away in a Manger'?"

"Listen, I grew up right down the road from 'Oh Little Town of Bethlehem' and I still don't know a single verse."

"I want him. We need him. It's boring being with the same bunch of people all the time."

So they called Saleh and he said he would come—"thrilled" was the word he used. He wanted to ride the bus to their house, he didn't want anyone to pick him up. Her father muttered, "He'll probably forget to get off." Saleh thought "caroling" meant they were going out with a woman named Carol. He said, "Holiday spirit—I was just reading about it in the newspaper."

Susan said, "Dress warm."

Saleh replied, "Friend, my heart is warmed simply to hear your voice."

All that evening Susan felt light and bouncy. She decorated the coffee can they would use to collect donations to be sent to the children's hospital in Bethlehem. She had started doing this last year in middle school, when a singing group collected $100 and the hospital responded on exotic onion-skin stationery that they were "eternally grateful."

Her father shook his head. "You get something into your mind and it really takes over," he said. "Why do you like Hamadi so much all of a sudden? You could show half as much interest in your own uncles."

Susan laughed. Her uncles were dull. Her uncles shopped at the mall and watched TV. "Anyone who watches TV more than twelve minutes a week is uninteresting," she said.

Her father lifted an eyebrow.

"He's my surrogate grandmother," she said. "He says interesting things. He makes me think. Remember when I was little and he called me The Thinker? We have a connection." She added, "Listen, do you want to go too? It's not a big deal. And Mom has a *great* voice. Why don't you both come?"

A minute later her mother was digging in the closet for neck scarves, and her father was digging in the drawer for flashlight batteries.

Saleh Hamadi arrived precisely on time, with flushed red cheeks and a sack of dates stuffed in his pocket. "We may need sustenance on our journey." Susan thought the older people seemed quite giddy as they drove down to the high school to meet the rest of the carolers. Strands of winking lights wrapped around their neighbors' drainpipes and trees. A giant Santa tipped his hat on Dr. Garcia's roof.

Her friends stood gathered in front of the school. Some were smoothing out song sheets that had been crammed in a drawer or cabinet for a whole year. Susan thought holidays were strange; they came, and you were supposed to feel ready for them. What if you could make up your own holidays as you went along? She had read about a woman who used to have parties to celebrate the arrival of fresh asparagus in the local market. Susan's friends might make holidays called Eddie Looked at Me Today and Smiled.

Two people were alleluia-ing in harmony. Saleh Hamadi went around the group formally introducing himself to each person and shaking hands. A few people laughed silently when his back was turned. He had stepped out of a painting, or a newscast, with his outdated long overcoat, his clunky old man's shoes and elegant manners.

Susan spoke more loudly than usual. "I'm honored to introduce you to one of my best friends, Mr. Hamadi."

"Good evening to you," he pronounced musically, bowing a bit from the waist.

What could you say back but "Good evening, sir." His old-fashioned manners were contagious.

They sang at three houses that never opened their doors.

They sang "We Wish You a Merry Christmas" each time they moved on. Lisa had a fine, clear soprano. Tracy could find the alto harmony to any line. Cameron and Elliot had more enthusiasm than accuracy. Lily, Rita, and Jeannette laughed every time they said a wrong word and fumbled to find their places again. Susan loved to see how her mother knew every word of every verse without looking at the paper, and how her father kept his hands in his pockets and seemed more interested in examining people's mailboxes or yard displays than in trying to sing. And Saleh Hamadi—what language was he singing in? He didn't even seem to be pronouncing words, but humming deeply from his throat. Was he saying, "Om"? Speaking Arabic? Once he caught her looking and whispered, "That was an Aramaic word that just drifted into my mouth—the true language of the Bible, you know, the language Jesus Christ himself spoke."

By the fourth block their voices felt tuned up and friendly people came outside to listen. Trays of cookies were passed around and dollar bills stuffed into the little can. Thank you, thank you. Out of the dark from down the block, Susan noticed Eddie sprinting toward them with his coat flapping, unbuttoned. She shot a glance at Tracy, who pretended not to notice. "Hey, guys!" shouted Eddie. "The first time in my life I'm late and everyone else is on time! You could at least have left a note about which way you were going." Someone slapped him on the back. Saleh Hamadi, whom he had never seen before, was the only one who managed a reply. "Welcome, welcome to our cheery group!"

Eddie looked mystified. "Who is this guy?"

Susan whispered, "My friend."

Eddie approached Tracy, who read her song sheet intently just then, and stuck his face over her shoulder to whisper, "Hi." Tracy stared straight ahead into the air and whispered "Hi" vaguely, glumly. Susan shook her head. Couldn't Tracy act more cheerful at least?

They were walking again. They passed a string of blinking reindeer and a wooden snowman holding a painted candle.

Eddie fell into step beside Tracy, murmuring so Susan couldn't hear him anymore. Saleh Hamadi was flinging his arms up high as he strode. Was he power walking? Did he even know what power walking was? Between houses, Susan's mother hummed obscure songs people hardly remembered: "What Child Is This?" and "The Friendly Beasts."

Lisa moved over to Eddie's other side. "I'm *so excited* about you and Debbie!" she said loudly. "Why didn't she come tonight?"

Eddie said, "She has a sore throat."

Tracy shrank up inside her coat.

Lisa chattered on. "James said we should make our reservations *now* for dinner at the Tower after the Sweetheart Dance, can you believe it? In December, making a reservation for February? But otherwise it might get booked up!"

Saleh Hamadi tuned into this conversation with interest; the Tower was downtown, in his neighborhood. He said, "This sounds like significant preliminary planning! Maybe you can be an international advisor someday." Susan's mother bellowed, "Joy to the World!" and voices followed her, stretching for notes. Susan's father was gazing off into the sky. Maybe he thought about all the refugees in camps in Palestine far from doorbells and shutters. Maybe he thought about the horizon beyond Jerusalem when he was a boy, how it seemed to be inviting him, "Come over, come over." Well, he'd come all the way to the other side of the world, and now he was doomed to live in two places at once. To Susan, immigrants seemed bigger than other people, and always slightly melancholy. They also seemed doubly interesting. Maybe someday Susan would meet one her own age.

Two thin streams of tears rolled down Tracy's face. Eddie had drifted to the other side of the group and was clowning with Cameron, doing a tap dance shuffle. "While fields and floods, rocks, hills and plains, repeat the sounding joy, repeat the sounding joy..." Susan and Saleh Hamadi noticed her. Hamadi peered into Tracy's face, inquiring, "Why? Is it pain? Is it gratitude? We are such mysterious creatures, human beings!"

Tracy turned to him, pressing her face against the old wool of his coat, and wailed. The song ended. All eyes were on Tracy and this tall, courteous stranger who would never in a thousand years have felt comfortable stroking her hair. But he let her stand there, crying, as Susan stepped up firmly on the other side of Tracy, putting her arms around her friend. And Hamadi said something Susan would remember years later, whenever she was sad herself, even after college, a creaky anthem sneaking back into her ear, "We go on. On and on. We don't stop where it hurts. We turn a corner. It is the reason why we are living. To turn a corner. Come, let's move."

Above them, in the heavens, stars lived out their lonely lives. People whispered, "What happened? What's wrong?" Half of them were already walking down the street.

ABOUT THE AUTHORS

TONI CADE BAMBARA published her first story at the age of twenty as a student at Queens College. She is the author of several collections of short stories, including *The Sea Birds Are Still Alive* and *Gorilla, My Love*, and a novel, *The Salt Eaters*. She lives in Philadelphia.

DUANE BIG EAGLE was born in Claremore, Oklahoma, and is of Osage descent. He has been writing poetry and fiction for twenty years, and his work has been published in the United States and abroad. His books include *Bidato*, *Theme for Ernie*, and *Birthplace: Poems & Paintings*. Duane Big Eagle teaches in the American Indian Studies Program at San Francisco State University. He currently lives in Petaluma, California.

ROBERT CORMIER is a former journalist and the award-winning author of *The Chocolate War*, *I Am the Cheese*, *The Bumblebee Flies Anyway*, and *Beyond the Chocolate War*. He was born in Leominster, Massachusetts, where he still lives. He has four grown children.

LANGSTON HUGHES was born in Joplin, Missouri in 1902. His first published work appeared the year after his high school graduation. After that he wrote many stories, essays, plays, poems, and songs. His works of poetry include *The Weary Blues* and *The Dream Keeper*; his short-story collections include *Simple Speaks His Mind* and *The Ways of White Folks*. He led a colorful and adventurous life, traveling as a seaman to Europe and Africa, living in Paris and in Harlem, where he was at the center of the Black Renaissance. He described his life in his two-volume autobiography, *The Big Sea* and *I Wonder As I Wander*. Langston Hughes died in 1967.

GISH JEN's real first name is Lillian, but in high school friends nicknamed her "Gish" after the actress Lillian Gish. She is the author of many short stories and a novel, *Typical American*. She lives in Cambridge, Massachusetts.

FRANCISCO JIMÉNEZ was born in Mexico. When he was four years old, his family came to Santa Maria, California to work in the fields as migrant workers. At the age of six he joined them on the migrant circuit, attending school only when the harvest season was over in November. When he was fifteen, he was deported to Mexico, but he returned two months later and went on to graduate from high school with honors, to receive scholarships to college, and to become a United States citizen. Francisco Jiménez is now a scholar, a university professor, and the author of short stories and books of literary criticism. "The Circuit" is based on his childhood experiences. He lives in Santa Clara, California.

ANNE MAZER, the editor of *America Street*, grew up in Syracuse, New York in a family of writers. She grew up in the only Jewish family in her neighborhood, which became the subject of her recent novel, *Moose Street*. She attended art school, lived and studied in Paris, and worked in New York City before becoming a writer. Among her other books are the novel *The Oxboy* and *The Salamander Room*, a picture book. She lives in northeastern Pennsylvania with her husband and two children.

MARY K. MAZOTTI was born in California in 1924. Her parents were immigrants from a Calabrian village, and she spent her childhood among Italians who came from the same area. She is the mother of seven children. For many years, she worked as a school secretary. In 1981, she began to write, and has been published in various journals.

NICHOLASA MOHR was born in New York City's El Barrio. She began her career as a graphic artist. Her books include *In Nueva York*, *El Bronx Remembered*, *Felita*, and *Going Home*. She lives in Brooklyn, New York.

TOSHIO MORI was born in Oakland, California in 1910. He is the author of two collections of stories, *Yokohama, California*, which was the first collection of short stories published in the United States by a Japanese American writer, and *The Chauvinist and Other Stories*, and a novel, *Woman from Hiroshima*. During the Second World War, he was camp historian at the Topaz relocation center in Utah. He died in 1980.

LENSEY NAMIOKA was born in Peking, China and has lived and traveled all over the world. Her family moved to the United States during the Second World War, when she was nine years old. Sent to school before she knew any English, she learned about American culture and language from scratch. She is the author of many books, including *White Serpent Castle*, *The Samurai and the Long-Nosed Devils*, *Who's Hu?*, and *The Phantom of Tiger Mountain*. She says that she is "descended from a long line of eager eaters, and her books (and stories) always describe food in loving detail." Lensey Namioka and her husband live in Seattle, Washington.

NAOMI SHIHAB NYE grew up in St. Louis, Missouri; Jerusalem; and San Antonio, Texas, where she now lives with her husband and son. She is an honored poet whose work has appeared in many collections and anthologies. Her books of poems are *Different Ways to Pray*, *Hugging the Jukebox*, and *Yellow Glove*. She is also the editor of a children's anthology of poems from around the world, *This Same Sky*. She will soon publish her first picture book, about her grandmother in Palestine.

GRACE PALEY was born in the Bronx, New York. She is the author of many stories and poems. Her books include *The Little Disturbances of Man*, *Enormous Changes at the Last Minute*, and *Later the Same Day*. She has taught at Columbia University, Sarah Lawrence College, Syracuse University, and City College of New York. She lives in Vermont and New York City and is an activist in the anti-nuclear movement.

GARY SOTO was born in Fresno, California, which is the setting for his story "The No-Guitar Blues." He writes both poetry and narrative prose. Among his books are *The Tale of Sunlight, Baseball in April and Other Stories, Taking Sides, Living Up the Street,* and *Pacific Crossing.*

MICHELE WALLACE was born in the Harlem section of New York City, the daughter of artist/author Faith Ringgold and the pianist/master printer Earl Wallace. She is a professor of English and Women's Studies at the City College of New York and the City University of New York Graduate Center and the author of two books, *Black Macho and the Myth of the Superwoman* and *Invisibility Blues.* Her story, "Sixth Grade," describes an experience she had with a teacher that resulted in her leaving that school. Michele Wallace writes, "Curiously enough, although the episode was painful to remember . . . after I wrote the story, not only wasn't the memory painful anymore, I could barely recall the details without consulting the printed story. I think writing helps to heal our wounds."

ACKNOWLEDGMENTS

"Raymond's Run" by Toni Cade Bambara, from *Gorilla, My Love* by Toni Cade Bambara, copyright © 1972 by Toni Cade Bambara. Reprinted by permission of Random House, Inc.

"The Journey" by Duane Big Eagle, copyright © 1983 by Duane Big Eagle. Reprinted by permission of the author.

"President Cleveland, Where Are You?" by Robert Cormier, from *8 Plus 1* by Robert Cormier, copyright © 1980 by Robert Cormier. Reprinted by permission of Pantheon Books, a division of Random House, Inc.

"Thank You, M'am" by Langston Hughes, from *The Langston Hughes Reader*, published by George Braziller, Inc. Copyright © 1958 by Langston Hughes, copyright renewed 1986 by George Houston Bass.

"The White Umbrella" by Gish Jen, copyright © 1984 by Gish Jen. First published in *The Yale Review*. Reprinted by permission of the author.

"The Circuit" by Francisco Jiménez, copyright © 1973 by Francisco Jiménez. First published in the *Arizona Quarterly*, Autumn 1972. Reprinted by permission of the author.

"La Ciramella" by Mary K. Mazotti first appeared in *The Dream Book: An Anthology of Writings by Italian American Women*, edited and with an Introduction by Helen Barolini, copyright © 1985 by Helen Barolini. Reprinted by permission.

"The Wrong Lunch Line" by Nicholasa Mohr, from *El Bronx Remembered: A Novella and Stories*, copyright © 1975 by Nicholasa Mohr. Reprinted by permission of HarperCollins Publishers.

"Business at Eleven" by Toshio Mori, from *Yokohama, California*, copyright © 1949 by Toshio Mori. Copyright renewed 1976. Reprinted by permission of The Caxton Printers, Ltd.

"The All-American Slurp" by Lensey Namioka, copyright © 1987 by Lensey Namioka. Reprinted by permission of Lensey Namioka and her literary representative, Ruth Cohen, Inc.

"Hamadi" by Naomi Shihab Nye, copyright © 1993 by Naomi Shihab Nye. First published in *America Street*, by arrangement with the author.

"The Loudest Voice" by Grace Paley, from *The Little Disturbances of Man* by Grace Paley, copyright © 1956, 1957, 1958, 1959 by Grace Paley. Reprinted by permission of Viking Penguin, a division of Penguin Books USA Inc., and the author.

"The No-Guitar Blues" by Gary Soto, from *Baseball in April and Other Stories*, copyright © 1990 by Gary Soto. Reprinted by permission of Harcourt Brace & Company.

"Sixth Grade" by Michele Wallace, copyright © 1974 by Michele Wallace. Reprinted by permission of the author.